A MENDOCINO MYSTERY

MARY CESARIO WEAVER

LOST
COAST
PRESS
Fort Bragg
California

A Mendocino Mystery
Copyright ©2003 by Mary Cesario Weaver

For information, or to order additional copies of this book, please contact:

Lost Coast Press
155 Cypress Street
Fort Bragg, CA 95437
(800) 773-7782
www.cypresshouse.com

Cover note: The cover features the statue of "Father Time and the Maiden," which was carved from a single redwood log about 1866 and sits atop the Masonic Temple on Lansing Street in the village of Mendocino.

Cover Design: Chuck Hathaway / Mendocino Graphics

Library of Congress Cataloging-in-Publication Data
Weaver, Mary Cesario, 1946-
   A Mendocino mystery / Mary Cesario Weaver.--
1st ed.
   p. cm.
   ISBN 1-882897-74-9 (alk. paper)
   1. Women private investigators -- California -- Mendocino--Fiction.   2.Mendocino (Calif.)--Fiction.
3. Witnesses--Fiction. I. Title.
   PS3623.E385M46 2003
   813'.6--dc21   2003001784

MANUFACTURED IN THE USA
4 6 8 9 7 5

MIX
Paper from
responsible sources
FSC® C011935

Acclaim for
A MENDOCINO MYSTERY

"Not so disturbing it will give you bad dreams, this murder mystery by a North Coast author mixes up the right combination of characters—adolescents and adults, good guys and bad guys and it all takes place in the familiar Mendocino Village. It's got sex, drugs and not too much gore."

—The Press Democrat, *Santa Rosa*

"*A Mendocino Mystery* is a fun read! People come into Cheshire searching for this book, a one-of-a-kind, behind-the-scenes intrigue that captures a spicy slice of Mendocino life."

—*Linda Rosengarten, Cheshire Bookshop, Fort Bragg*

"I have just found a new favorite author...Weaver writes in the first person without the character's showing the slightest self-consciousness that comes out so often in this style. The protagonist's wit is bold without being strong-well, a little. Suspense builds from one query to the complexities behind it. As each detail is pursued and the solution lurks just around the corner—Wham! It is snatched away. The heroine is placed in danger, survives and keeps up the pursuit. The villain is not the one you suspect. I am very selfish and demanding of authors whom I discover and enjoy. I want them to write more, more, more! Weaver says she is, indeed, considering another Syracuse story."

—*Jo Campbell, Willits News*

EVEN MORE ACCLAIM!

"A nifty page-turner...tidy little mystery...pegged to Mendocino County and, loosely, our very own Brink's truck robbery...Mary gets just right the lurking menace behind the jolly façade of Mendoland."

— Anderson Valley Advertiser, *Boonville*

"Whether you're a 'local' or a traveler, you'll want to put aside enough time to finish this book once you start it. I dare you to try putting it down! Weaver captures the color and spirit of the coastal town while spinning a riveting tale of murder and mayhem. Highly recommended."

— *Diane Honeysett, Toyon Books, Healdsburg*

"The perfect read — a very enjoyable, light mystery by a local author, with a likable young woman sleuth."

— *www.BookCrossing.com*

"First rate mystery...lively, funny, fast paced... jammed with local color...just the right escape reading for your Mendocino vacation."

— *Linda Pack, Gallery Bookshop, Mendocino*

To my daughter,
Kirsten,
and my granddaughter,
Cali Etna

Special thanks to Mendocino resident and author Kathleen Cameron, for her unrelenting encouragement and constant support in getting this book to press.

Big hugs also to Lilla Woertendyke, my best friend since high school, and my daughter's godmother, for more than forty years of comfort and advocacy.

Accolades also to Joan Curry, for all her efforts to safeguard the buildings and character of the village of Mendocino.

A MENDOCINO MYSTERY

CHAPTER 1

It was Monday, December 2, close to ten o'clock on one of those mornings when the coffee wasn't working. If it didn't perform, how the hell was I supposed to? Nothing could press me into action today, except for old layers of Catholic guilt. Blatant signs of venial sins of omission filled my office, loose ends I'd refused to tie the last few weeks, while in hot pursuit of a swindler who doubtless now wished I'd never been conceived.

Office plants, all gifts from naïve friends, had no business in this infertile and unwholesome atmosphere. Frequent droughts occur when I'm working on a case; even now, however, between cases and with ample time on my hands, I refused to bring them water from a sink three steps away to slake their parched little stems and leaves.

I could hear their plaintive plant plea, curled, yellowing leaves and brittle roots calling me a lazy, sadistic bitch. From their potted perspective, maybe I am, but I prefer to focus on my strong side: when working on a lead, how the adrenaline pumps through me like fuel-injected, high-octane jet propellant, driving me through eighteen hour workdays for weeks at a time, until—Bingo!—I drop the final and winning piece onto the table. Then I collapse in pleasurable exhaustion, followed by days like today, when it doesn't matter how much coffee I drink or how much guilt I conjure up; nothing will work until the next investigative challenge enters my bloodstream.

I'm a forty-three-year-old retired journalist turned private investigator, the happily divorced mother of a nineteen-year-old college sophomore who changes her major every week and has no idea what she wants to be when she graduates—besides a professional shopper.

My name is Syracuse, after my hometown in upstate New York. When I was an undergraduate venturing out west for the first time to attend Arizona State University, friends started calling me that because I practically lived in an old gray Syracuse University sweatshirt with the bright orange school insignia across the front. It was the sixties. Everyone was changing their names to fit the dreams, or psychic flashes, as they were known then, of the flower children. I thought Syracuse beat the hell out of Stumbling Fawn or Slippery Feather.

Of Italian extraction, brought up in the Italian neighborhood in Syracuse, I was raised on the Columbus Bakery's hard-crusted white bread and Carmen Basilio's hot pork sausage. My hardcore Catholic parents served fish on Fridays, imposed mandatory confession every Saturday at the Cathedral of the Immaculate Conception of the Blessed Virgin Mary, and put the fear of eternal damnation in me were I to eat meat on a Friday or die before confessing my latest sins.

Every Sunday morning at Mass, as I slowly made my way up the aisle to take communion, I faced the perpetual dilemma of whether I'd gone too far with my boyfriend Saturday night, thus invalidating my earlier confession. For added insurance, I always recited a quick Act of Contrition as I knelt at the altar rail, gazing upward and praying like crazy that the cardboard communion wafer, which always stuck to the roof of my mouth like nothing else I had ever put in it, was being absorbed by my clean soul.

Adding to my discomfort was my conviction that Joe Pannetti, the altar boy who held the gold plate under my chin lest I drop the sacred wafer onto the sanctuary floor, had a bulge in the front of his pure white robes—a direct result of staring at my quivering tongue, which he had been French kissing hours earlier, as we bumped and rubbed Catholic body parts in the backseat of his '57 Chevy.

That was a long time ago. My youth may be over, but that doesn't leave me old and drab. Subtle makeup does wonders: a little eyebrow plucking here, a touch of mascara there, a monthly hair enhancement—okay, a dye job—but I don't use that pancake makeup old ladies use; that I save for the griddle, with extra maple syrup.

After years of composing on a 1946 Royal typewriter, during the pre-word-processor days and darker ages of journalism, I discovered that I could make a lot more per hour as a P.I. than I could per column inch as a reporter. Besides, it was more exciting to be an integral part of the unfolding story than just another correspondent taking notes in a newsroom miles away from the action. Sure, in the early days my sleuthing caseload wasn't the material movie producers fought over. I had to take what came, usually husbands wanting to know whom their wives were screwing on the side, or vice versa.

After years of experience, I now have the luxury of choosing the cases I want to pursue, whether for financial reasons or just the pure intrigue when one arouses my catlike curiosity. No new clients had called for appointments this morning, so I was surprised to hear a knock on my front door. I was grateful, however, for the interruption of the debate between my superego and id on whether to water the goddamn plants.

Slowly, reluctantly, due to this morning's inertia, I rose from my chair and walked to the door. Whoever was on the other side wasn't going to win the patience award this morning: a second and third series of knocks resounded before I could reach for the knob. Turning it, I swung the door no more than six inches toward me before a breathless woman dashed through the narrow opening and quickly closed the door behind her.

Paranoia seemed to fire from every cell in her body. Her eyes looked like she was hallucinating: she was surrounded by simultaneous visions of Godzilla and King Kong, and didn't want Fay Wray's part in the script. If she was paranoid, I couldn't believe she'd burst into my office like that. It's no secret most people don't run to private investigators at the first sign of terror; usually, they're strongly inclined to run in the other direction.

"Are you Syracuse?" she asked.

Good going, I thought, at least you found your way to the right place, but it also indicated I would soon be reading for my part in her horror film.

"Yes."

Hearing this single word, she slumped into the chair beside my desk, put her hands over her face, and sobbed for several moments, during which I studied her. Late thirties, maybe forty, she was dressed in what used to be called collegiate fashion: pleated, plaid wool skirt in tones of gray, white, and maroon, a matching maroon cardigan sweater over a solid white blouse. Despite a little gray around the temples and a few wrinkles near her mouth and eyes, she still had the look of a perennial sorority girl.

Even tense and drawn, her features maintained their attractiveness, a Grace Kelly kind of all-American beauty, shoulder-length blonde hair, and lovely eyes.

She had dough, too, and not the Columbus Bakery variety. You could tell from her perfect teeth, expensive gold and leather accessories, and the air of elegance that curled around her like velvet smoke rings. She had a quality about her that took enormous expense to maintain, as if her well-bred genes had always been spoon-fed and clad in nothing but designer products.

I asked my little damsel in distress how I could be of help to her.

4

"I'm very embarrassed about it, but quite frankly, I'm scared to death. I swear I'm not usually like this—afraid, I mean. The past few days have been extremely difficult for me. I'm a very stable woman under ordinary circumstances, but something extraordinary has occurred and, well, now everyone thinks I've lost my mind," she said.

In my imagination, my eyes rolled back in my head, but my words said otherwise: "Well, why don't you run it past me and see what I think, but first, can I offer you a bottle of mineral water or some tea?" I said graciously.

I decided coffee wasn't the drink of choice here: she was already stimulated enough; her energy had jolted me into high gear as if I'd just mainlined six cups of strong java.

"Mineral water is fine, thank you," she said.

I reached into the small fridge I keep under my worktable and pulled out two bottles of local mineral water with natural lime flavoring. I handed her a bottle along with a glass. She was definitely not the type to drink anything out of a bottle under conditions short of a natural disaster. From what I could surmise, it seemed her idea of roughing it would be enduring a slow bellhop at the Ritz.

When we were settled with our drinks, I said, "Let's start with your name."

"Anne. Anne Spencer Phelps."

"O.K., Anne, you're embarrassed, frightened, usually play with a full deck, but something happened and now everyone believes you're losing your mind," I said, using my best impression of the famed psychologist Carl Rogers, feeding back her own lines.

Lowering her eyes and voice, she said, "Yes, that's right."

"So, what happened?"

"I witnessed a robbery." The tension in her speech was rising again, like a delicate spring inside her was slowly being stretched taut, and her greatest fear was whether her mind would snap when the spring recoiled. I waited for her to compose herself before asking her to continue. She took several deep breaths, fidgeted, rearranged herself in the chair, and then proceeded with her terrifying report.

"I was driving up Little Lake Road on my way home when I saw one of those armored trucks that transport money for banks parked on the side of the road. Two men with guns were next to the truck, taking moneybags out the rear door. Another man, in a uniform like guards wear, was lying on the ground, face down in some grass near the truck."

"Sounds good so far. Go on."

"Naturally, I didn't know what to do, I mean, I didn't stop because I thought for sure they would shoot me, so I drove home and called the sheriff." With this, she again lowered her face and began to cry, a quiet, almost childlike whimper.

"What happened next, Anne?"

"The sheriff said he would get right on it, but he never called back. I thought maybe he was busy arresting them or something, so I waited until the next morning to call him again, and he said there'd been no report of an armored truck robbery anywhere near here."

"I see. No wonder you're upset. What was the name of the deputy you talked to?"

"Ed Nelson."

I knew Ed. Skillful and thorough, he'd been with the department for over ten years, and rarely missed a beat in the crime-solving tune, as long as he stayed away from drugs, which as far as I knew, he had for the past year.

I hesitated a moment, then asked, "When did you see this, ah, robbery take place?" I was afraid to use the term "alleged" because I wanted Anne to trust me, to feel that I wasn't questioning her reality and was aware and protective of her fragile emotional and mental condition. As a seasoned journalist, it was an arduous task not to use the ass-covering adjective that managing editors continually shoved down your throat for fear that the "innocent until proven guilty" would sue the shit out of your paper for libel.

"It happened on Saturday afternoon on my way home from the village, probably around five."

"Did they see you?" I asked gently.

"I don't know. Maybe. That's why I'm so afraid."

"Have you talked to anyone else about this?"

"My father. He thought it was someone filming a movie. My husband agrees with him."

"Did you see any cameras or other movie equipment?" I asked encouragingly. "You know, anything to indicate that perhaps this is a possibility?"

"No."

"Did you see anything else, anything at all that seemed peculiar?"

"There was an old red pickup truck parked in front of the other truck. I assumed it belonged to the robbers, but I didn't get the license number because I was afraid to slow down."

"The movie angle sounds feasible," I said, a note of optimism in my voice. "You may have overlooked the camera if you were looking intently at the truck and everything else that was going on, and you did say you didn't slow down, so there wasn't much time to take everything in."

"No. That's not possible. I called Harriet Ross, who books all the movies, television shows, and commercials up here, and she said there's been no filming involving the use of an armored truck." More tears and fidgeting transpired before Anne could continue. I sustained my supportive, consoling role, feeling, as I often do, more like a therapist than a detective, because the two professions are more similar than different. My problem-solving techniques, however, utilize external events rather than the internal struggles between unconscious desires and ego-controlled impulses, unless, of course, I'm working with a bona fide psychopath.

"Look, Anne, give me a couple of days to check out my sources and see what I can come up with. There's got to be an explanation. I can see you're a strong, mature woman, and not just making this up because you're bored and there's nothing good on TV." I said, in an attempt to humor her and stabilize her hysteric condition.

"My father can be so mean," she said, holding back the insistent tears. "He implied I was crazy or imagining the whole thing, and said I should just forget about it. Do you know how awful that makes me feel? I saw a crime, a hideous one," she exclaimed with just a touch of anger in her voice.

"I'm really sorry this is being so hard for you, Anne. I believe you. I'll help you put together the pieces of the puzzle, as bewildering as it may seem to you right now," I said, even though I half suspected she was a woman with too much imagination and too little control of herself.

"Is there anything else you would like to know?"

"I nodded and said, "Yes. Where exactly on Little Lake Road did this happen?"

"At the three-mile marker there's a small turnout on the right side of the road as you head east. It was right there."

"I'll go out there this afternoon, and call you as soon as I know something. Now, I'll need a retainer from you: I charge fifty an hour plus expenses, so five hundred will be enough to start; if I can wrap this up today I'll send you back the balance. Give me your address and phone number too."

Her address and phone were printed on the check she handed me, which was made out in neat cursive writing, indicating she probably got A's in handwriting all through grammar school—unlike me, who finally had to resort to printing, or face a life sentence in Miss Schaefer's third grade classroom.

I stood up and escorted Anne to the door, while she thanked me for being so kind and listening to her ghastly account. I assured her she was not alone, that the majority of my clients had similar emotional responses on their initial visits to a private investigator's office. She seemed pleased and comforted to hear this. Her splendid face was now relaxed, almost serene in its beauty. I felt like I'd performed a miracle on her psyche, subdued her anxiety with a verbal tranquilizer that didn't require ingestion in pill form.

Her exit was bland compared with her dramatic entry. My eyes followed her down the stairs to the street. She moved like a dancer, softly and with ease, stopped to look both ways before crossing the street, and entered a blue Mercedes sedan parked on the ocean side of Main Street.

I turned and walked back into the office. Seated at my desk again, I typed up notes of our conversation while it was still fresh in my memory, noting all the pertinent details, including Anne's emotional affect, as if I were a therapist trying to deduce which personality disorder she was suffering. As a detective, I give as much weight to a person's comportment as a shrink does, knowing that a client's facial expressions often convey messages with stronger and more significant meaning than spoken words. I'm also a staunch believer in Freudian slips, and often analyze them in my practice, but Anne hadn't revealed any of those inadvertent and sometimes entertaining errors.

Anne's account seemed plausible. As an intelligent and seemingly stable woman, however, it was obvious she didn't appreciate a good mystery when she was required to be part of the production, especially cast as the unbalanced and mystified blonde. More than anything, she needed reassurance from someone in a professional position—that's why she'd retained me.

I put the notes into my wall safe, reset my answering machine, and prepared for the drive to the scene of the alleged crime. I rummaged through the closet for my camera and close-up lens. As an undergraduate art major back in the 1960s, I had become a good photographer, never knowing, when I was shooting aesthetically pleasing compositions, that the skill would be invaluable in procuring evidence in my later days as a crack P.I. Coincidentally, during these same years I became an excellent marksman on the shooting range, another asset in my sometimes dangerous profession, when self-defense calls for a Smith & Wesson rather than a Pentax. I grabbed two rolls of black-and-white film and stuffed all the paraphernalia into a leather camera case.

One undeniable fact about Anne's peculiar case stood out: I was hooked by the bait she had dangled. Most of my cases are routine investigations with cut-and-dried solutions. This one, on the other hand, offered intriguing possibilities. Without that tempting lure, I wouldn't have felt so compelled to leave my comfortable office and race out to the scene.

My earlier mood, dripping with satisfying lethargy, had been replaced by an exhilarating enthusiasm, one of the cheap thrills I list in the assets column of my balance sheet each month. Just before I reached the door, I noticed neither Anne nor I had touched our mineral waters, so I poured both bottles over the thirsty plants, recited three quick *Hail Marys*, and stepped outside.

CHAPTER 2

Walking down the single flight of stairs to the street below, I was reminded of how fortunate I was to have office space in the village. Since Mendocino has become such a popular haven for tourists in recent years, the majority of available commercial space, even residential properties, has been converted into cushy, expensive gift shops and vacation rental homes for city folks seeking fresh air, abundant parking, temporary ocean views, and time out from their upwardly mobile treadmills.

Fortunately, Lucia Rosa, a friend who owns a fashionable women's clothing store on the first floor of my building, offered me her upstairs storage room for an office. Although small, having survived the tedious remodeling stage, it now features breathtaking panoramic views of Big River, the bay, and the vast Pacific Ocean, through a pair of dormers on the west wall, and French doors opening out to a deck on the sunny south side.

The village has 500 year-round residents, tops, with another 1,000 staying over nightly in some fifty hotels and bed and breakfast inns. Several hours north of the San Francisco Bay Area, Mendocino nestles above steep and treacherous cliffs over the rough, frigid sea, and along the mouth of Big River, which forms a natural fishing harbor. Fishing and logging were the only industries along the coast, until tourists discovered the quaint New England-like ambiance and began to spend millions on their transient pleasures—a nice percentage of it emptying into hungry county coffers through sales and bed taxes.

I discovered Mendocino's charm about twenty years ago during an extended, meandering vacation. I was going through a miserable divorce, didn't want to go back to the Southern California town I was living in—it wasn't big enough for both of us to live any kind of civilized existence—and was searching for Utopia, USA. It was love at first sight, a welcome relief from the hell-on-earth state a divorce can provide. The white clapboard buildings, picket fences, Victorian architecture, refreshing sea breezes, and native pines reminded me of New England; I felt like I'd finally come home.

It's only fair to add that I also fell in love with someone the very day I first set foot on Mendocino soil, and that weighed into my decision, even though the affair was over after a short but respectable period. My infatuation with the area has never waned, as most romances do in these days of disposable relationships.

I popped my head into Lucia's store below. She was busy dressing Chloe, a wonderful old art deco mannequin, in one of the latest fashions, something purple, soft, and flowing. I'm no connoisseur when it comes to women's apparel—jeans and sweaters are my garments of choice—but Lucia has it down to a refined, tasteful, and appealing science.

"I'm going out for a few hours, wondered if you could pass that on if anyone comes by the office?" I announced in a brisk, businesslike tone.

"Do I look like Della Street? I'm trying to run a business here, a clothing store, in case you haven't noticed," Lucia fired back in her classic velvet hammer style.

She usually gave me a hard but not serious time at first, just to remind me I wasn't God's gift to her world, but I knew her next line would be as soft as the rayon dress she was now carrying over to the window display.

"But you're cute, so I'll do it," she added, just a hint of a warm smile beginning at the corners of her mouth.

"Thanks, kiddo. I'll talk to you when I get back. Kind of in a hurry now, see you in a little bit."

My Volvo station wagon was parked right in front. Ah, one of the joys of country living: ample parking. Several tourists strolled along the wood plank sidewalk, swinging colorful shopping bags with local stores' logos printed in tasteful, trendy letters. Browsing at a leisurely pace in their designer jeans, Topsider deck shoes, and stylish leather jackets, they professed a relaxed air equal to their peaceful surroundings.

Mendocino wasn't always so pristine and quaint. Back in the late 1800s this very Main Street consisted mostly of saloons, and the village was much like the gold rush towns so often portrayed as wicked places of drunken brawling, lewd overtures, and raucous manners. The only difference was, the gold came in the form of logs.

Many of the townspeople were offended by the loggers' morals and the saloon owners' attitudes. Even when Mendocino had a population of about 1,000—it's gone down over the years, due to conversion from residential to commercial usage, and families moving farther out (but still within the sphere of influence)—it boasted thirty saloons, or one bar for every thirty-three and a third men, women, and small children.

Repeat business was guaranteed by the custom of giving change in metal tokens, made to look like coins, with the name of the bar and GOOD FOR ONE DRINK stamped on them. This practice kept the drinking man from taking home the full amount of his meager wages. The family of a man with a heavy thirst suffered, I imagine, emotionally as well as financially. Prostitution also entered the rowdy scene: Mendocino's first hookers were Pearl Peck and Big Lil, whose names I adore, and slip them whenever I can into an appropriate conversation with friends.

In 1908, the citizens of Mendocino, outraged by the offenses to the moral character of the village, voted by local option to outlaw saloons and alcohol in town—prior to the nationwide Prohibition, which didn't come along until 1920—and didn't repeal the law until the end of Prohibition in 1933. Saloons were either converted into grocery stores or other businesses, or simply closed their swinging doors.

The county covers over 3,500 square miles, extending inland from the coastline, with rugged, mountainous terrain and imposing scenic valleys sprinkled throughout. The "dry" loggers around the turn of the century didn't have to venture too far to quench their thirst: Fort Bragg remained "wet" and was only seven miles north. At the same time in Mendocino, which was at one time referred to as the "Italy of the New World," numerous Italian hotel owners were frequently caught serving wine to guests who said they "could not live without it." By the time prohibition was enforced throughout the state, bootleggers came on the scene in the county as well as everywhere else in the nation.

The county's harsh topography has always had a reputation for being tough country, inhabited by equally tough individuals whose lifestyles had a raw and crusty quality. Loggers and the subsequent bootleggers possessed this individualism, this frontier spirit, which was a necessity for survival in the area.

The logging industry, active again today, declined in the 1950s, and a severe depression followed. Land became virtually worthless until the late 1960s and '70s, when the unwanted property found eager new buyers from the cities: the generation of flower children who wanted to move to the isolated county and become completely self-sufficient, raise their own food, cook and heat without electricity, and raise their children in an unpolluted environment.

Many of these families, already using marijuana recreationally, took advantage of the abundant inexpensive acreage to not only produce pot for their own consumption, but to make it a means of earning a living in an economically depressed area. In addition to these original mom-and-pop growers, more pot farmers moved to the area, and production and pot prices soared. What began as a single-family plant progressed to cottage industry levels, and finally, mass production of a new strain of marijuana, with the highest level of the mind-altering ingredient THC ever marketed. Paraquat spraying of Mexico's pot crops added to the local growers' delight and pocketbooks, as buyers were afraid to smoke the tainted Mexican weed. Despite many citizens' negative attitudes toward marijuana cultivation, it was a boom to the depressed economy.

Other changes quickly followed. More growers, who were not peace-and-love-oriented hippies, but hardened criminals, entered the scene, as did thieves who robbed farmers of their expensive crops at gunpoint. Bullets flew often enough that it became dangerous to take a leisurely stroll or horseback ride through many areas of the county, for fear one would be mistaken for a pot thief. Law enforcement agencies put the heat on to cut down on pot growing. It wasn't unusual back then to spot a sheriff's wagon parked in front of the Mendocino Bakery, while a deputy took a coffee break, leaving dozens of enormous marijuana plants in full view in the locked carrying compartment in the back of his vehicle.

Despite the crackdown, marijuana is still grown and harvested throughout the county to this day, in part because Mendocino County has one of the highest rates of unemployment in the state, and many otherwise honest, law-abiding members of the community still depend on their crops to make it financially. Even some of the more affluent residents, like teachers and healthcare professionals, supplement their mediocre wages by growing just a few plants—if their names were ever published in the local paper, it would astound many of the more straight-laced citizens. The market price of high-quality pot remains very profitable; although it requires a lot of stamina and just pure guts to continue to grow it today, many are still willing to take the risk to reap the benefits.

More than one village business now operating as a cushy new enterprise, which will no doubt be frequented by the same tourists who just strolled past me, was opened using cannabis-growing profits for start-up money. The issue of "to grow or not to grow" is philosophical, but today I have other dilemmas to face, like getting out to the scene of the latest alleged crime, only a fifteen-minute drive from the village.

I made a note to myself to stop by the sheriff's office on the way back to check out Anne's story with Ed Nelson. I backed my car out and headed for Little Lake Road, which originates as Little Lake Street in the village proper, running west to east. Once across the main coastal highway, it turns into a country road winding through redwood forests dotted with wild rhododendrons.

The area appears uninhabited, since all the homes are hidden several yards off either side of the road, down unobtrusive narrow dirt driveways sheltered by thick forest. I forged ahead through the woods, wondering what this journey must have been like for the Indians who lived here hundreds of years ago, when the land was teeming with wildlife, rich in clean streams and fresh air, and a solitude that will never be captured by the modern traveler. Even though the area is still regarded as rural, I'm offended by the electrical lines strung through the tall branches, and the millions of cubic yards of black asphalt punctuated with an iridescent yellow center stripe.

The three-mile marker is precisely that: a small white highway sign with the numerals 3.00 printed sideways on it—another modern intrusion. I pulled over onto the dirt shoulder just shy of the turnout, not wanting to disturb any previous tire marks or other evidence. It hadn't rained for several days—always a possibility in this area—and this part of the road wasn't close to resembling a main thoroughfare, so there was a good chance the turnout was used infrequently, and the odds of finding undisturbed potential clues in my favor.

I walked slowly to the dirt clearing, immediately noticing a series of tire tracks: duals on the rear, one bald. The tracks entered the turnout, jerked and twisted when the brakes were applied more than casually, and then reentered the road at the far end of the turnout. Crisscrossing them just as they exited was another set of tracks, these running perpendicular, as if another vehicle, smaller and lighter by the faint impression left by its tires, had parked sideways, blocking the larger one.

I went back to my car, got my 35mm camera, and shot several black-and-white photos of the tracks, including a series using my close-up lens on the tread patterns.

Combing the surrounding area, a task I relish—the real nuts and bolts of detecting, as opposed to the less gratifying parts of the job description, like typing up the reports—I inched my way around the turnout's oval contour, gradually stepping farther out of the egg shape in approximately three-foot increments. The sparse dry grass was only about six inches high, making it easy to spot anything if there was anything to find besides pine needles and, for crying out loud, several cigarette butts. Smokey the Bear would turn grizzly at this discovery: there were six of them, fresh, Camels sans filters. Using a pair of tweezers, I slipped them all into a small plastic bag. They hadn't been tossed out by any unconscious motorist with pyromaniac tendencies; each was crushed flat, more in the category of the venial, as opposed to the mortal division of forestry sins.

Someone stood here for at least six smokes. If it takes approximately five minutes to finish each cigarette, he or she had lingered here for at least half an hour while waiting for something or someone to show up.

Just to the right of the oval I was currently tracking, an object foreign to the forest's greens and browns caught my attention. I bent over and picked up a small gray cap with a shiny black plastic visor. Although it bore no emblem, it resembled the hats guards wear with matching uniforms, only this one was very flimsy material, almost like a theatrical prop.

Well, Sherlock, you sure solved this one quickly, I thought. One of the movie companies must have been filming out here, after all. Anne must not have checked out all the studios that shoot here. This might be good news and a relief to her, but for me it meant a fifteen-minute investigation, or a grand total of $12.50 in wages for the day, and no chance of riding off into the sunset as a big-time heroine on a sleek white horse. Despite my find, I decided to stop by the sheriff's station. Careful not to disturb the tire tracks, I flipped a U-turn and headed back toward the village.

In the incorporated areas of the county, police forces govern, but rural shenanigans are under the auspices of the sheriff's department. The closest substation is a few miles north of Mendocino on the coastal highway. The structure is one of the oldest buildings on the coast, still preserving its western flavor, constructed out of honest-to-God redwood logs, interlocked at the corners, just like the Lincoln Logs from which I derived infinite girlhood joy assembling pioneer fantasies. A hitching post and rail still stand in front of the nostalgic site. Each time I pull my car in to rest, its bumper next to the rail, I expect to see horses hitched there, rather than the line-up of green-and-white sheriff's cruisers.

Usually, one deputy is assigned to station duties, while others patrol up and down the coastline. Most of them aren't particularly generous about giving me information or assisting in my investigations, even if they overlap with their own cases, but I have one pal at the station whom I've helped several times over the years, in professional as well as personal capacities.

I was relieved to see him as I walked in the heavy front door that some ambitious carpenter had constructed out of two-by six, tongue-and-groove vertical boards supported by four enormous brass hinges. Ed was sitting behind the front desk, feet propped up, reading the sports section of the morning *San Francisco Chronicle*. He had played minor league ball for several years, and could still quote the batting averages of even the most obscure players in the majors. Approaching forty, Ed maintained his athletic build, religiously working out at the gym. He had muscles in places where most men don't even have places, but without the grotesque globs of an overachieving body builder.

Ed usually greeted me with virile yet lighthearted energy, but today he seemed evasive, withdrawn, and intent on remaining absorbed in his newspaper. His face was drawn and his eyes bloodshot. He looked like he'd just pitched eighteen innings with no rest or food to sustain him. Without taking his eyes from the paper, he finally mumbled, "Hey, Syracuse, how are those Orangemen doing?"

"I don't follow them anymore, Ed." I answered in a stern, irritable tone. "My daughter and I have gone through a dozen institutions of higher learning between us, so my allegiance has shifted through every color in the college football rainbow. I've graduated to the pros now, the 49ers to be precise, unless you want to talk baseball and my beloved Giants" I said, hoping to engage him, draw him out of his tight, guarded position.

"I doubt you came by just to talk about baseball," he said in a clipped, self-effacing manner.

"You're right. I've got this client, thinks she saw an armored truck being held up on Little Lake Road. She said she talked to you." I decided to keep the conversation on a business level, get the information I needed, then blast him later with a little attitude-adjustment bomb.

"Oh, yeah," he said, still refusing me any eye contact, "I talked to her. Real nervous type, scared out of her wits. I made out a report, checked out the banks and armored truck service, came up with zilch."

"Did you go out to the, ah, scene?"

"Didn't think there was any reason to." I decided not to mention the cap I'd found, not yet, anyway.

"Yeah, well, if there wasn't a robbery, I guess there isn't much point in going any further with this, but if you do hear anything more, I'd appreciate a call."

"Sure."

Okay, smart-ass. I knew Ed thought I would leave now, having completed our business, and I could sense the urgency in him for me to do just that. Instead, I loaded both barrels and prepared to open fire on his guarded stance.

"Let's cut the shit, Ed. I don't have to ask you where you've been or what you were doing, because it's written all over your face, you creep—cocaine," I said, unloading my first round.

Still refusing to look at me, he scanned the empty office to be certain no one was listening to my critique of his present situation. I'm about as sensitive as a bulldozer when I confront friends who remind me of how thin and delicate is the tightrope that a druggie walks.

"You've been clean a whole goddamn year. What the hell did you do, decide to go out and celebrate?"

"I fucked up," he muttered. "My ex and I got into one of our battles and I'm working double shifts. I'm tired, for Christ's sake."

"Brilliant. O.K., I'll help un-fuck you. You're my friend, Ed, one of my best friends. I'm no Mother Theresa, but when you get off work, go get yourself a decent meal somewhere. I'll pick you up at your place at seven-thirty and we'll do a hot tub, even though I certainly have a million other things I could do tonight."

"I'm sorry, Syracuse. I didn't want you to know," he said timidly.

20

"Well I do, so cut the sentimental crap. I'll see you in a couple of hours."

I gave him a little pat on the shoulder and a quick kiss on the cheek. Frustrated, I turned and left the office, feeling like a wounded animal seeking comfort in some cave. I settled for the sanctuary of my Volvo. Driving back toward the village, I tried to sort out my feelings. I'd come on strong with Ed, and probably should have stayed longer and talked with him about his problems, but I felt irritated and not in as compassionate a mood as I should have been. Maybe in a couple hours I'd be in a better place to talk with him and be more supportive.

I've lost too many friends to drugs over the years, and the last thing I want to see is Ed's name on the obituary page of the *Mendocino Beacon* because he got wasted and drove into a telephone pole or overdosed on some drug he decided to experiment with.

I pulled into the same parking place I had vacated earlier, and stuck my head into Lucia's store. "Any messages, my little pimento?" This particular endearment originated when Lucia named her store The Last Pimento, in hopes that clients like Lauren Bacall and Humphrey Bogart would frequent it. I think it sounds more like the name of a bar than a boutique.

"No, Perry," she said brusquely.

"Nice talking to you," I replied with a little wave of my hand. I could see she was busy with a customer, so I headed upstairs.

Next, I called Harriet Ross, the agent who books all the films on the coast; she wasn't in, so I left a message for her to call me at home. It was five o'clock. I'd missed lunch, and I was hungry and tired. The emotional scene with Ed had drained the charge Anne had thrust into my system earlier. Where to go from here was the question. What the hell did a fake cap, real tire tracks, and a bag of cigarette butts represent? I didn't want to think about it anymore. Home and food sounded like the sanest moves to make next.

I glanced over at my plants before I left the office. They seemed to be standing up a bit straighter—amazing what a little carbonation can do for the soil.

(HAPTER 3

I live fifteen minutes south of the village, give or take an overloaded, slow-moving log truck or two. A remodeled tool shed bigger than a breadbox but smaller than a two-car garage, my cabin sits in a grove of virgin redwoods, some up to five feet in diameter, lending a sense of strength and comfort to my refuge from life's irksome and stress-provoking contests.

Mr. Tank greeted me at the door, delivering a series of meows on various pitches from his eighteen-pound bulk. Empty bowls are the pat complaint emanating from his pea-sized brain, its two-track system capable of focusing only on food or sleep.

I gave him a quick roughing up, stroking his long gray fur backwards from tail to head, then a delicate pass down his soft throat until a purr of appreciation vibrated through my fingertips. His bowl would have to be filled before any of my immediate needs could be considered. Utterly spoiled, His Tankness insisted on star-shaped dry cat food—none of those round "Cheerios" for him. He ruled the roost around here, never taking no for an answer. I let him get away with this arrogant behavior out of guilt for accidentally driving my car over him about three years ago.

The twelve-year-old neutered tomcat likes to meet me at the end of my driveway when I come home from work and give me a furry escort up to my parking place. One evening, during his nonchalant stroll, he stopped suddenly to scratch a flea. Even though I slammed on the brakes, there wasn't time to avoid the collision. I rushed him to the vet, where he spent two weeks in intensive care with only a fifty-fifty chance of surviving.

Once home after the incident, I began to spoil him by preparing gourmet meals and pretty much letting him have his way with me. Guilt, you see, will push a recovering Catholic into monumental compromises. Tank senses this and has never let me forget the tragic, and in his mind premeditated, occurrence.

It was cold. The fog had come in, dropping the temperature some fifteen degrees. I stepped back outside and walked over to a massive woodpile. I learned a long time ago—the hard way, as my mother insisted I always did—that you could never have too much dry wood in this moist climate. I pulled back a corner of the heavy plastic tarp and reached in for a small redwood log, placed it on a large oak round, and delivered several small blows with my lightweight ax, splintering it into a dozen small pieces of kindling. The act was impressive; even if it was the softest wood on earth to split, I still felt as strong and capable as Paul Bunyan. Chopping wood is excellent therapy on angry, foul days when release is mandatory and, as in this case, could also be turned into productive enterprise.

I stepped back into the cabin, crushed up yesterday's sports section, tossed the balls of paper and fresh kindling into my tin Lizzie, a cheap wood-heating stove that's nothing more than an oversized tin can, and dropped a lighted match into the chamber. Mr. Tank strolled over to the beckoning fire, paused to lick a front paw, his portable washcloth, wipe his face, then settle down in my favorite chair next to the stove to continue his bath.

I headed for the kitchen and my dinner, a large bowl of brown-rice krispies covered with sliced bananas and vanilla-flavored soymilk. My idea of a gourmet meal is to make reservations anywhere else. Home cooking is your basic crackers and cheese, pasta, or canned chili on colder nights. Most people would say that, nutritionally, Tank ate better than I did.

It was only six o'clock; mentally, I was still fresh. I thought I should place a personal ad in the local paper, searching for anyone who'd seen what looked like, or knew anything about, the alleged robbery. It was worth a try. I was writing myself a note to call the paper the next day during business hours when the phone rang.

It was Harriet Ross. I've known Harriet for twenty-five years, since we roomed together at Arizona State. I knew even when we were sophomores that Harriet, born with style and talent to match, could charm and churn her way to the top of whatever field she chose. English and boys were her dual major. She idolized and quoted the most intellectual yet sensitive writers of the day—especially her favorite, Theodore Roethke, from her home state of Washington—and dated the most handsome and popular frat guys on campus. Her ability to have her pick of the litter left the other coeds in awe and with a plethora of runts to select among.

After graduating in the late 1960s, Harriet moved to Hollywood to produce television commercials; she was tops in the business before she traded the fast track for a mellow rural lane about ten years ago, when the film industry began to show serious interest in the Mendocino Coast, which could pass for New England in movies requiring that setting, without the additional expense of shipping cast, crews, and equipment cross-country.

When Harriet moved to Mendocino she also became Lucia's business partner at The Last Pimento. A dynamic duo in the rag trade, their store is one of the most successful enterprises in the village. Harriet's current boyfriend, Larry, teams up with her to play occasional pinochle games against Lucia and me.

Possessing a slightly competitive edge, Harriet joined the health club with me, and we play a fierce racquetball game at least twice a month. She can usually outsmart me, but I can out-hit her, so we're comparable opponents.

My present case is indirectly related to Harriet's motion picture business, but I've brainstormed with her on other cases I've tackled because she has such a perceptive and probing mind herself.

"I know what you're going to ask," Harriet said as I picked up the receiver. "I've already talked to your client and to the cops. Nothing resembling your steel carriage has ever been used up here for a movie or commercial. With the winter rains approaching, the season's over for this year, too. I just wrapped up a Chevrolet commercial about two weeks ago, and that's it until spring. It took forever to finish it, with the on-and-off foggy drizzle we had. It's too hard to shoot a complete scene when it's sunny one day and gray the next—never enough continuity for this business. Larry and I are going on vacation for a couple of months, straight south until we find some sun."

"Yeah, I could use a little of that myself, the continuity I mean, or the sun for that matter. Say, Harriet, what's the chance of a small, independent freelance making this film with the armored truck and you just not knowing about it?" I asked enthusiastically.

"This isn't L.A., sweetheart. I'd know about it. Also, they'd need permits from the sheriff to shoot on public roads. Sounds like your client fantasizes on big trucks. If it were me, I'd come up with something more titillating than that," she answered in her smooth-edged Hollywood style.

"I'm sure you would." Changing the subject, I asked, "What about props and costumes, where can you buy those around here?"

"Only one place, over the hill, in Ukiah, a business called 'The Great Imposter.' They're open twenty-four hours; catch a lot of late-night prima ballerinas who like to dress up in tutus and hit the streets. They also have singing telegram service, and send employees out in some pretty outrageous outfits to sing at stag parties and things like that. They'd be open now, so you could give them a call tonight if you feel like you have to pursue whatever this intriguing case of yours is."

"Yeah, I think I will. Thanks for your help. It'll save me some time. You got any ideas?"

"Not a clue, darling."

"Well, don't run off on vacation before Lucia and I have a chance to whip you at pinochle."

"Don't worry, I'll give you plenty of notice. Let me know how your mystery turns out. I don't know how anything as big as an armored truck could be invisible to anyone but your client. Weird. Ciao."

I hung up and dialed information, feeling a remarkably small amount of guilt for not looking up the number in the nearby phonebook. Ukiah is the nearest town of any size, with a population of over 20,000. It's an hour and a half drive east over a series of rolling hills, along a twisting country road built in or adjacent to the old stagecoach route. Many sections of the road are still dirt and can get quite treacherous during the rainy season, when the clay surface turns into an unexpected ice rink.

On a spring day it's one of my favorite drives, scenic beyond Webster's ability to describe, meandering over hills and through valleys alongside a small river covered on both banks by canyon oaks and majestic redwoods that reach across the clear, bubbling stream to embrace one another's branches. Some of my best poetry has been attempted on that road when, seized by breathtaking beauty, I pulled over with pen in hand, prepared to unite momentarily with the collective poet's metrical soul.

A little past the halfway point to Ukiah is an old resort, Orr Hot Springs, named after the original owners, but now maintained by a community of individuals who are involved in a lifestyle that includes extensive vegetable and flower gardening, ecology, and holistic health practices. In the mid-1800s, many Indian trails radiated from these medicinal springs located in a deep canyon covering about forty acres. Stagecoach passengers used to bathe, then spend the night in the old hotel, which burned down many years ago, seeking health, relaxation, and relief from arthritis and rheumatism.

Today the baths consist of an eight-foot enclosed redwood hot tub, a small outdoor pool with a tiled bottom built into the rock, four claw-foot bathtubs in private rooms, a large swimming pool fed by both hot and cold mineral springs, and an adjoining sauna for those daring enough to jump into the cold water following a hot steam bath.

Guests may stay overnight, either in quaint redwood cabins with green trim on the windows and porch railings, or camp out in tents along the creek. Meals are prepared in a communal kitchen adjacent to a cozy dining room and lodge, where a warm fire and oversized couches and chairs welcome the weary traveler. The surroundings are also excellent for hiking, jogging, and making love, far removed from the stresses of everyday life. This sheer paradise is an inviting oasis in life's grim, arid desert. I try to plan my trips to Ukiah with ample time to stop for a soak and a few hours of lavish peace and quiet.

Feeling a little regret not to be making the drive over after reflecting on the beauty of the old road and the possibilities at the hot springs, I placed my call.

A young female clerk answered, "We can make your dreams come true. How can I help you?"

"Well, perhaps you can," I said. "Do you sell guard's uniforms and hats, in a gray shade?"

"Yes, we do, but we are presently out of them."

"Oh. Out of them. Are they real popular or something?"

"No. Not at all."

"Then why do you suppose you don't have any?" I asked, a little irritated.

"We only had two outfits, and they sat around for a long time, y'know, like, they were what we call slow movers."

"I see. Do you know who bought them, by chance?"

"Why do you ask?"

In this business you're sometimes better off telling a lie. This time I opted for the truth, for no particular reason other than not having a good quick line to feed her.

"I'm a private detective out of Mendocino; name's Syracuse. I'm working on a case that involves the possible use of such an outfit. Is that enough for you?"

"Oh. Just a moment and I'll check in the computer," she answered, putting me on hold. I let my mind wander back to the hot springs and what I might be doing there now if I'd chosen to drive to Ukiah rather than call.

"I'm sorry. All our records show is it was a cash sale made back on October sixth. We are not going to reorder them, because we had them for an awfully long time before they sold."

"Do you remember the hats very well?"

"I should—I dusted them enough times."

"What'd they look like?"

"Well, they were gray, with black plastic visors, and made out of a thin cotton; kind of cheap looking, if you ask me."

I thanked her and rang off. The few pieces of information I did get might or might not fit into one theory I was formulating. I suspected I was getting someplace, though just where, I wasn't sure. I walked back into the kitchen and put on enough water for one cup of coffee. While it was brewing I changed into something warmer: a heavy gray wool sweater over a tan turtleneck and beige corduroy pants.

I looked at my watch: seven-fifteen and time to leave. I gulped the coffee, damped down the woodstove so the fire would burn slowly and continue filling the cabin with warmth for my return in a couple of hours, whispered some sweet cat nothings into the sleeping fat feline's furry ear, and headed out the door to pick up Ed.

CHAPTER 4

The next morning, I strolled into my office with a warm blueberry-and-cheese Danish and a steaming cup of coffee from the Mendocino Bakery. At least once a week I force myself to indulge in a treat from the local bakery. My reasoning today was based on the principle of reward for services rendered the previous night to Ed, who was toughing it out, showing great determination in his battle to stay off drugs once and for all.

The office was exceptionally warm and bright this morning, the rays of sunshine streaming through the French doors matching the mood the pastry had already set in motion. The office is decorated in simple yet tasteful furnishings, thanks to Lucia's eye for style. I had insisted on a two-tone paint job, with pale rose walls and high-gloss, oyster white oil trim on the windows and doors. My desk, chairs, and worktable are all light gray, the same hue as the walls. A salt-and-pepper carpet seasons the prevailing color theme, and has the ability to conceal the everyday dirt tracked in — low maintenance, the salesclerk had stressed.

I stepped out the French doors onto the deck to savor my pastry and coffee while I looked out at the vast ocean before me. Today it was so still you could skip stones across it. I spotted several migrating whales when they swam to the surface and spouted tall fountains of air and water from their blowholes.

They were headed south to the Bay of Conception in Baja for their annual cavort in the warm southern waters, just as Harriet was planning to do.

An early caller knocked at the front door, disrupting my aquamarine reverie. Not another Fay Wray, I hoped. I walked back into the office, opened the door, and there stood the late Cary Grant.

Mid-sixties, handsome, tanned face with chiseled features, dark, heavy-framed glasses, and a full head of perfectly coiffed white hair, he wore a double-breasted gray flannel suit and a serious red-striped tie, like the kind that politicians sport. Black wingtips completed his outfit. I wondered if he knew that only one in 10,000 men ever wore suits in this neck of the woods.

"I assume you are Syracuse," he said in a condescending tone.

"Yeah, who're you?" I answered with as little show of politeness as possible.

"May I come in?" He entered without waiting for my reply. "My name is Frank Spencer. My daughter is a client of yours, Anne Phelps," he said.

"What business is it of yours?" My irrational dislike and distrust of men in suits inflamed me. My mood had suddenly changed from warm Danish to iceberg, and this guy was seeing only the tip of it. I must have had a traumatic experience with a suit when I was a kid, either that or something Republican-like was seeping through his perfectly tailored seams.

"I would appreciate a few moments of your time in regard to a serious matter."

"Okay, shoot." I didn't offer him a seat, might wrinkle his pants, but he seemed content standing.

"My family is going through a very difficult time. I do not know how much Anne has told you, but her mother has suffered a nervous breakdown and is currently hospitalized." He paused, waiting for my response, but I wasn't about to tell him anything Anne had or had not confided in me. Sensing this, he continued, "Anne is very upset over this development, and is herself teetering on the edge of insanity."

"So what does this have to do with me?" I asked, suspecting what was coming next from this highbrow.

"We believe it would be in the best interests of our family if you would just forget this incident Anne has reported to you. Our doctor concurs. It can only add to the enormous stress Anne is trying to cope with. I am sure you understand," he said in a commanding voice, as if I were a subordinate, part of the staff he probably dictated orders to every breathing moment of his pompous life.

"I'll think about it," I said, in a brash, non-reassuring tone.

"Of course you may keep the retainer she gave you for any trouble you may have already gone to," he added.

His businesslike tone, phony politeness, and absence of conversational contractions stirred up every antisocial part of my personality. Aristocratic bullshit: his use of the term "we" could only mean he kept a mouse in his monogrammed shirt pocket to make him a perpetual, self-contained couple.

"Does Anne know you're here, pal?" I fired back.

"Anne is not well enough to make this kind of decision right now. I am her father, and qualified to know what is best for her health," he said.

"Of course. I'll bet she speaks highly of you, too," I said, dripping sarcasm.

He turned on his heel and walked back to the door. Sharply now he said, "Consider this case closed, if you will. We no longer desire your services." With that proclamation he slammed the door behind him.

My fiery Italian instincts wanted to follow and kick him down the stairs like any decent Mediterranean would, but my more mature judgment restrained me. What the hell was going on here? This Cary Grant look-alike wasn't fiercely protecting his daughter; he was hiding something, and didn't want me gumshoeing around on his turf and whatever seedy secrets were buried in it. All he did was further rouse my curiosity about this case, unburdened with the baggage of respectability his world took for granted.

I was furious. I knew any move I made right now would be irrational and cause immeasurable grief later on. I couldn't believe I was able to control my temper for once and actually think before I reacted. Meekly, I called the local newspaper and placed my personal ad. I refrained from dialing Anne's number until I could become more rational. I did call Harriet to see if she could play an impromptu game of racquetball, but she wasn't home. Discouraged, I walked out to my car and decided to drive to the health club in Fort Bragg. Ten minutes later I was swimming laps in the tepid indoor pool. Then I took a cold shower and a hot sauna, followed by another cold shower.

Strenuous exercise is the best thing I can do for myself when I want to strangle someone; the health club has saved many a life. Christ! Legally, Cary Grant had no right to take me off this case. Anne was over twenty-one, and despite his wishes, he had no recourse and couldn't break our contract. Anne was not bordering on insanity as he had suggested. She might be a bit hysterical, but that was the extent of her neuroses.

Cooled off, I tried to call Anne from the pay phone in the health club lobby as I was leaving, but there was no answer. My ulcer was making a burning, nauseous demand to please remember lunch today. Compromises and antacids keep my delicate guts intact. Coffee is on the "avoid" side of every diet list my doctor hands me, but I figure if I cut it with extra half-and-half, things will work out in the acid war taking place just above my navel. Sometimes the settlement works, sometimes—like now—it doesn't. I blamed Frank Spencer for the inner rage gnawing at my raw ulcer.

I headed back to Mendocino. Unrelenting stomach pain, and guilt over this morning's rich Danish and strong coffee, prompted me to pull into the health food store when I reached the village. I decided to pick up a wholesome and bland selection of politically and nutritionally correct foods. I genuflected as I entered the store, housed in a turn-of-the-century church. Recently, someone had put a fresh coat of barn-red paint on the weathered siding, and trimmed the front doors with a pale blue-gray, shiny oil finish. In the early afternoon light, an enormous stained glass window behind the counter reflected rainbows throughout the store's interior.

I walked over to one of the dairy cases and drew out a ready-made sandwich built with avocado, tomato, and alfalfa sprouts on sprouted wheat bread. From another case I chose a bottle of organic apple juice. Then I returned the sandwich, deciding the tomatoes were too acidic for my ulcer and the avocado too high in fat for my cholesterol count. I placed the apple juice back on its respective shelf, noting that it too was acidic.

Shit. What the hell can I eat? I wandered over to the cracker section and selected a box of plain soda crackers, unsalted. To this I added a small container of low-fat cottage cheese and a banana. I also grabbed a tiny container of soymilk and then marched up to the counter with my miserable, boring choices, growling at the clerk as I plopped them down on the counter. She took my cue and said, "Hard day, huh?" and left it at that except to tell me the price of the goods.

"Don't take it personal. It's just a little hard for an Italian to give up the hot stuff for this kind of meal."

She smiled warmly at me and waved for the person behind me to move forward. The collective of individuals who own the store are a lively and entertaining group, but today I wasn't interested in enjoying their lives or mine, at least not while I was wallowing in self-pity because of my limited food options—as if they were a form of celibacy and I the world's horniest consumer.

Spencer was the culprit. I might have been able to withstand an Italian sausage sandwich at Reitano's Restaurant if it hadn't been for his attitude and the effect it had on me. Slitting his red-striped throat still sounded like a pretty good idea.

I drove out to the headlands overlooking the Pacific to eat my exciting lunch while I tried to soothe my agitated mind. The workout at the club had actually helped, but I wasn't fully willing to admit it yet. I saw another pod of whales heading south and began to yearn for their freedom and peaceful lifestyle on the planet. The ocean was very comforting for me, probably because I'm a Cancer, a water sign, and generally hit the water when the going gets tough. After finishing the last of my lunch, I turned the car around and decided to drive out to Anne's house and confront her directly to see if she was indeed coming unwrapped, as her father had implied.

My journey took me three and a half miles beyond the now infamous three-mile marker on Little Lake Road, using the address on Anne's check—which I still hadn't deposited in my account—as a navigational tool. Two rural mailboxes at the entrance to a gravel driveway announced SPENCER on one, PHELPS on the other. I concluded Anne and her husband lived on or near the same land as Cary Grant. I turned in the drive and went up a passage just wide enough for a single car for nearly a quarter mile before the house came into view.

It was an enormous redwood mansion with a lot of glass and a high, steep roof punctuated with a half dozen oversized skylights. A second-floor balcony ran the length of the building. Two smaller buildings, one I guessed to be Anne's home, and the other a guesthouse, were designer placed on either side of the main structure. All featured redwood tongue and-groove horizontal siding, with black trim on the windows and doors. At the far end of a pasture stood an old red barn, looking like an Iowa transplant or the last remaining vestige of the original forty-acre homestead. Several deer grazed in the pasture.

I parked in the circular driveway in front of one of the smaller homes and walked up to the front door. A tiny brass slot over the doorbell, a miniature picture frame, held a small piece of heavy paper that said PHELPS on it. I rang the bell, waited, rang again, waited some more, and then proceeded in the direction of the main house. There were no cars in sight, so I figured the entire complex was deserted, unless there was an auto-less housekeeper.

I walked over to the mansion, careful not to brush against the ring of sharp holly bushes that encircled the house. I sensed an energetic gardener was in Spencer's retinue, since the landscaped grounds reflected sustained care and boasted a full array of colorful flowers despite the late time of the year. Red-hot pokers, yellow and orange calendulas, pink, white, and red impatiens, and the last of the roses teetering on their extended branches just before they tip, were blooming. Straw flowers, stiffly resilient, still managed to look alive.

The mansion's impressively heavy oak door had a stained glass center panel of a bird of paradise; the doorbell next to it also featured a nameplate, only this one read SPENCER. Certain he wasn't there, unless he had ridden in on one of the deer, I boldly rang the bell. Receiving no answer, I rang it a second and then a third time.

Finally, I heard the sound of footsteps slowly making their way down a flight of interior stairs. Probably a very old housekeeper, and I hadn't even taken the time to figure out what lie I was going to tell to cover for why I was here in case Spencer got wind of my visit. I held my breath and at the same time tried to take a deep breath as the handle turned.

CHAPTER 5

The door was opened slowly and cautiously by a disheveled young man in his early twenties, who looked like he'd just woken up in the back of a freight car after traveling across the country curled up in the straw with a herd of dairy cows. His clothes were rumpled, obviously slept-in, his face unshaven, and his hair hadn't decided yet which direction it was headed, shooting off in several, some straight up. He reeked of marijuana and urine.

"Who're you?" I asked, so surprised at the sight of him that I forgot I was supposed to be concocting a lie.

"Who're you?" he fired back, crouching a little bit behind the door.

"I asked first," I said firmly.

"What the fuck do you want?" he snapped angrily.

The slob didn't scare me one bit. I knew I could blow him over and out like a cheap birthday candle with barely a flicker of flame left in it. "I'm a friend of Anne's. I'd like to speak with her, shithole, and she doesn't seem to be next door." My disposition hadn't improved much since my earlier encounter with Cary Grant, and now this kid was pushing me even farther into unbridled hostility.

"Well, she ain't here."

"I can see that. Mind telling me where I can find her?"

"Who the fuck *are* you, anyway?"

"I'm bored with these lines, buddy. I'm a private investigator. Name's Syracuse." I handed him one of my business cards. He stuck it in the hip pocket of his jeans. They looked like they'd stand by themselves once he stepped out of them—if he ever did. "Anne hired me to do some work for her. You must be the kid brother she talked to me about." A flagrant lie, but I had to find some way to engage this loser.

"What'd she say about me?" he asked in a serious tone.

"That your mother dressed you funny," I answered, poker-faced.

"You're a wiseass for a woman, you ever been punched out?"

Cary Grant must be real proud of this offspring. A throw-back, I'm sure he'd say.

"You really scare me, pal. Tell me where Anne is or I'm gonna call the health department and have you declared a public health nuisance for skipping your Saturday night baths."

With a scowl on his filthy face he said, "You're a real fuckhead, did you know that? Anne's gone for a few days, I don't know where." This guy's vocabulary was so impressive I wanted to choke him with a dictionary, but at least we were beginning to make some headway, and probably having about as meaningful a dialogue as he was capable of.

"Where's her husband?"

"He went with her," he said, with a grimace. He was beginning to slouch, as though he'd been standing upright too long and would topple over if he couldn't get back to a horizontal position soon enough.

"And Pop?"

"He's at work, I suppose. He didn't go anywheres, if that's what you mean." His grammar sent shivers up my spine, like fingernails across a blackboard.

I plunged ahead with my line of questioning: "You know anything about the robbery Anne saw, that involved an armored truck?" No reason to leave now, maybe the guy was on a roll and had more to spill from his stoned guts.

"No," he answered flatly.

"Next time you feel like having a chummy talk, give me a call. Number's on the card," I said, a broad smile spreading across my face.

"Fuck off," he said, slamming the door.

"Same to you, buddy," I managed to get in.

Nice little family scene we have out here. The daughter is a cooperative, reserved witness; dad's a patriarchal prick ruling over a dysfunctional, to put it mildly, brood; mom's apparently incarcerated in a mental ward for any number of psychoses, and sonny-boy's a fucking, to use his terminology, major pothead. Harriet Ross won't be shooting any sequel to the Brady Bunch with *this* all-American family.

I drove back down Little Lake to the village, stopped at the post office to pick up the mail, and headed over to my office. I was suddenly overcome with exhaustion. Spencer's arrogant attitude, blended with his son's insolent outlook, was enough to drain anyone of life force. I was no exception, despite my unlimited skills and endurance after many years as a private detective.

As I pulled up in front of my office, I could see Lucia sitting behind the counter in her store. I walked over to the front door and poked my head in. "How's it going in the clothing world today?" I asked.

"Oh, hi, Syracuse. Are you coming in? Haven't really talked with you in days," Lucia said, "Except for your brief check-ins; without them I'd think I was creating an illusion."

I walked in, stepping around the counter to an inviting couch—a store fixture for tired and bored husbands to occupy while their wives tried on clothes. A magazine rack stuffed with local publications advertising current events as well as most of the tourist-oriented businesses along the coastline stood at the far end of the couch. I collapsed into the soft, overstuffed cushions and threw my legs up over the low arm.

"Why don't you just make yourself at home?" Lucia quipped, just a touch of sarcasm in her voice.

"Sorry, Lucia. I've been in a rage all day, and now I'm so tired I can barely keep my eyes open.

"It's okay. I'm closing up. Stay put."

I sunk further into the cushions. A hand-held mirror was propped on top of the magazine pile. I picked it up and looked at my tired features. My brown eyes were glassy and had big dark bags under them. About half of my ponytail had slipped out of its holder and was cascading down the back of my neck and around my ears. I noticed an enhancement was past due: a rather large shock of gray hair was growing out in the front again, just to the left of my widow's peak. My mother used to say the peak foretold early widowhood. I imagine getting divorced in my late twenties was close enough to fulfill that particular prophecy.

I ran my finger across a few new wrinkles I spotted at the corners of my mouth, as if touching them would either make them dissolve or become more real if a second sense was called in to confirm what my eyes had discovered. I looked over at Lucia behind the counter and said, "That was a mistake."

"It's never a sign of brilliance to look closely into a mirror at our fragile age, my dear," she answered. "We keep that in here so women can look behind themselves in the full-length mirrors, certainly not to gaze in from the front."

"Christ, we're not even old yet, and I'm already beginning to understand why someone would get a facelift. In another year, at the rate I'm going, my face is going to look like the Sahara after a hard rain followed by a heat wave."

In a retail trance while she filled out the deposit slip, Lucia managed to look over her glasses at me, a smug look on her face.

"That isn't the kind of sympathetic gaze I expected after baring my soul to you, Lucia," I said brusquely.

"Sorry. I was happy to see how we finished today. Believe me, Syracuse, you look fine to me, although you *are* putting on a little weight around your middle."

"Great—one more thing to worry about."

"Get off your trip. I have to run this deposit over to the bank. Do you want to go out somewhere and get a bite to eat? I haven't talked with you in so long, I've almost forgotten who you are."

"Sure."

Lucia turned off the store lights and came over to the couch. She reached for my hand. All I wanted to do was remain curled up for about a solid week of uninterrupted sleep. Reluctantly, I put out my hand and let Lucia pull me up into a standing position and maneuver me out the door.

It was six o'clock. Darkness had enveloped the village, and the fog had come in thick and wet. Although the mist was chilly, it had an invigorating and cleansing effect on my jumbled, sleepy mind. The quiet streets were devoid of tourists as we made our way up Main and turned north onto Lansing. I noticed most of the Main Street merchants had the Christmas decorations up in their display windows, showing off their wares around pine boughs and fake snow.

Two skateboarders took advantage of the empty sidewalks, and charged down the other side of the street at a breakneck velocity that would have sent their mothers into cardiac arrest if they could have seen the daring antics, jumps, and turns executed with death-defying joyful precision. When I was their age I too was convinced death was something for old people. Skateboarding is illegal in Mendocino, but show me a cop who could catch these rascals at the speed they travel, unless he blew into town in a Batmobile.

Lucia dropped her deposit in the outdoor, after-hours drop

box in front of the bank, and we crossed the street to the Seagull Inn. Set into the front door was a stained glass panel of a seagull in flight, protected by two steel push bars so inept tourists or forgetful locals didn't propel their limbs through the delicate glass.

Entering from the cold fog, the warm air radiating from the dining room was an instant comfort. The tables were covered with burgundy tablecloths and white cloth napkins. Shiny silverware glowed in the light provided by white candles in little red holders that looked like votive candles from the Catholic Church.

The hostess led us to a small table for two on the west wall, near a window framed in tiny Christmas lights the shape and color of red peppers. We took off our jackets and draped them over the backs of our chairs before easing into them, or at least eased as much as one can onto a hard-backed, regulation restaurant chair.

Lucia had been quiet during our walk, but settled in, she now began her nightly harangue on the pitfalls of running a retail shop in a tourist town.

"Tedious, that's what they were today; had to be cajoled and encouraged and complemented on every last thing they tried on. And do they show any appreciation? Hell, no. They don't even have the decency to put things back on hangers, much less back on their respective racks. Assholes. Tedious assholes."

"For crying out loud, Lucia. You merchants have about as much right to complain as Liberace had. I see you all walking up to the bank with your deposits every night, laughing all the way."

"Don't start in, Syracuse, or you can have this joint to yourself," she snapped back.

"It *does* go with the terrain, you know. Part of the retail gig is waiting on people hand and foot, whatever the hell *that* means."

Lucia studied me for a moment before she responded. "What it means is, I work damn hard for money in this town."

"I didn't say you didn't. I'm just pointing out that you shouldn't bite the hand that feeds you, dear."

"Let's talk about something else. This topic is making me irritable. What are you going to order?"

"I think I'll just get a bowl of soup and a dinner salad."

"I'm going to get the same, unless the soup is that disgusting excuse for clam chowder they promote."

Lucia was really on a roll tonight. I wanted to tell her about the two jerks I'd spent my day with, but at this point I wasn't sure she was capable of hearing me. It sounded like she'd had her share of rude, obnoxious people for one day.

Something caught my attention when the hostess passed by our table with two men in tow. Suits. They were wearing suits. Peeking over the menu, I caught a glimpse of the first man: it was Cary Grant. I didn't recognize his companion, a short, skinny man whose large nose somehow reminded me of Templeton the rat from the E. B. White novel, *Charlotte's Web*. The hostess seated them several tables away from us, and behind a wooden partition, blocking my hopes of further scrutiny.

"Do you know a woman named Anne Spencer Phelps?" I suddenly asked Lucia.

She looked up for a moment and answered, "Does she look like an aging sorority girl?"

"Yeah. A combination of Ivy League and Grace Kelly."

"A serious shopper is what she is, but we don't carry much that really fits her style—y'know, kind of tailored."

"What's she like?"

"Well, she's outgoing, pleasant, kind of prissy, though. Looks great in blue, with those eyes of hers."

The waitress interrupted my subtle line of questioning. After we'd ordered, I looked over at Lucia in the candlelight and paused a few moments before continuing. Her silver hair glowed in the soft lighting, and her dark eyes had begun to relax, as if her earlier grumpy mood had lifted, perhaps momentarily sidetracked by my casual interrogation.

I looked at Lucia intently, caught up in my probing mind and its demanding curiosity, and whispered, "Do you think she's crazy?"

"Who, the waitress?"

"No, for Christ's sake, Grace Kelly."

Lucia shook her head back and forth and breathed a heavy sigh before she spoke. "How the hell am I supposed to know that? I'm running a women's clothing store, not a detective agency, and certainly not a mental health clinic."

"You know what I mean. What's your take on her?"

"I doubt from the little I've seen of her that she's a certified psycho, but to tell you the truth, Syracuse, I'm not so sure you're wrapped very tight these days yourself."

CHAPTER 6

Gentle raindrops drummed a soothing rhythm on the roof when I woke up the following morning. I peered out the north window at the gray drizzle falling in the forest behind my cabin. Deep puddles had formed in their usual places, so I knew the first serious downpour of the season had happened during the night. I can sleep through any natural loud noise, like cat disputes or log trucks downshifting on the curve out in front of my place; only when danger creeps or leaps within earshot do I stir, so I'd missed the steady, soothing downpour.

A heavy weight, however, rested on my chest: a warm Tankness, who, now sensing that I was more or less officially awake, began to stir and stretch his enormous bulk, which reached from my neck almost to my knees if you counted his furry tail. He gave his head a few quick shakes, as if trying to jerk himself out of a deep cat dream world and enter the reality of what we both knew came next.

I walked into the small kitchen, put on water for coffee, and heard Tank's thunderous thump as he jumped off the high bed and bounded for the kitchen to begin pestering me with painful-sounding cries for breakfast. His food was temporarily stored in the refrigerator, since a raccoon had recently discovered the cat door and the inviting roadside café within. The masked intruder was capable of opening cupboard doors, unscrewing jar lids, tearing into boxes, and creating food havoc that made the tiled kitchen floor resemble one of those supermarket aisles news photographers always shoot right after earthquakes. The coon hadn't yet figured out how to open the refrigerator, so I stored basic essentials in it now—like cookies and cat food.

The local humane society loaned me a special trap to catch and relocate the ring-tailed bandit; so far, I had managed to trap five of the neighbors' domestic cats—one twice—and a skunk. For now I'd given up my trapper identity and was formulating new designs for the cat door, instead. These included fantasies of a device that operated like an automatic garage-door opener, with a sensing mechanism attached to Tank's collar that would activate the cat door to open whenever he, and only he, stood in front of it.

Pouring my first cup of coffee was Tank's cue to moan more pathetically, even though he had just finished his dry stars. He knew the container of half-and-half was on the counter, and it certainly wouldn't hurt, in his opinion, to put a little taste on a saucer for someone as grand as he. Just so he'd know who was boss, I poured some into my coffee first, then gave him his share.

After living on the north coast for twenty years, I've grown to understand the rain's distinctive rhythms. This morning's indicated steady rain on and off all day, so I dressed accordingly in wool pants and sweater. After filling my thermos with two extra cups of coffee to drink in the car on the way into the village, I snagged my raincoat and wool hat as I went out the door.

Before going to the office I stopped at the post office to get the mail; I got a copy of this morning's local paper from the newsstand in front of the P.O. to see if my personal ad had appeared. I proceeded further up Ukiah Street to the bank to deposit Anne's check in my account. Although there are several banks over the hill in Ukiah and a few more in Fort Bragg, ten minutes north, Mendocino has only one, the Bank of Mendocino, in the heart of the village, at the intersection of Ukiah and Lansing streets. Extensive remodeling increased its size to accommodate the needs of a small community, yet it retains the charm and character of the earlier structure. Tourists love to take pictures of the historic building.

I rarely found it necessary to actually enter the bank, and I suspected banks were encouraging other customers to opt for the same move—using the ATM for most transactions would cut back on payroll expenses. Anne's check was drawn on the same bank I had my account with, and I wanted to check with a teller to be certain there were funds to cover it in case Daddy decided it was in Anne's best interests to stop payment on it. I walked over to the only teller I recognized, a woman whose daughter had graduated from the local high school with mine.

"Good morning, Syracuse. How are you?" she asked.

"Fine, Mildred, just wanted to know if you could run this check through the computer to be sure there are sufficient funds behind it."

"Sure, no problem. It'll just take a second." She took the check to a terminal behind her, pushed a few buttons, read the screen that was too small for me to sneak a peek at, and returned to the window. In a voice so low I had to lean forward to hear her, she said, "You don't expect the president's daughter to be writing bad checks now, do you?"

"What do you mean?" I exclaimed.

"Anne Phelps. She Frank's daughter," she whispered, as if it were of some significance.

"What are you driving at, Mildred?"

"Frank Spencer. He's the president of this bank. Didn't you know that?" she offered with a puzzled expression.

"No. No, I didn't." I tried not to show alarm or even the slightest concern on my face at hearing this unexpected news, though it was generating so many simultaneous thoughts that

I couldn't comprehend even one of them coherently.

"Did you need anything else, Syracuse?" Mildred said, snapping me out of the whirling trance in which I'd found myself suddenly regressing to my childhood in upstate New York, feeling like I was stuck in one of the old revolving bank doors with the thick black rubber pads on the bottoms that used to send waves of paranoia through me. Getting swept under one of those massive doors rated high on the same list that included being sucked down the bathtub drain.

I took this signal from my unconscious to mean that I was on to something. Intuition was trying to break through and assure me that I was on the right track, and would be a fool to jump off the speeding train before it could pull into the station.

"Yes. What's he like? Her dad," I managed to mumble in a somewhat composed voice.

"Oh, he's a very nice man. Has treated us real fair so far. He's only been here about six months, you know, transferred from a bank in Los Angeles when Mr. Lipari retired." She lowered her voice again; I thought I'd have to crawl over the counter to hear her. "Lately, though, he's been acting troubled, you know, since his wife has been sick, but that's only to be expected, you know."

"Yeah, I understand. Thanks, Mildred." I turned and started to leave the teller's window when she called after me.

"Syracuse, didn't you want to cash or deposit this check?"

Shit. I was so perplexed I had forgotten why I'd come into the bank in the first place. "Guess early senility is setting in, Mildred. I'd like to deposit it. Thanks for reminding me." I filled out a deposit slip, handed it to her, thanked her yet again, and left, feeling like I'd just come out of the spin cycle of an exceptionally vigorous washing machine.

By the time I'd run a few more errands, it was nearly one o'clock when I reached my office. Frank Spencer continued to mystify me. I wanted to connect his attitude and profession to the armored truck Anne might or might not have seen. Bewilderment is not a virginal state for me, but this was a different variety, and even more puzzling because so many aspects of this case seemed to be of an illusionary nature.

I glanced through my stack of mail: nothing inspirational there, unless utility bills were considered enlightening to things other than standard light sockets. I unfolded the newspaper, flipped to the classified section, and spotted my ad near the top of the outside column, an excellent location to grab even those readers who only scan the ads. My answering machine was blinking at me like a miniature crossing light. I pushed PLAY and an anxious male voice identified himself as Billy Spencer, the unkempt young man I'd spoken with out at the palatial Spencer estate. Now I knew his name, and he said he was Anne's brother, so my guess had been correct. He said he had something "fucking important" to talk to me about. The syntax further confirmed his identity. Billy wanted me to meet him at Big River Beach at noon. Damn—that was over an hour ago!

Deciding to chance that he might still be there. I dashed out the door and down the stairs, gave a quick wave to Lucia, who was changing her window displays again to keep the goods from fading in the light, jumped into my car, and headed for the beach. If it wasn't raining and I wasn't in such a big hurry, I would have taken the fifteen-minute walk down to the beach, along a beautiful trail carpeted with magnificent wildflowers. My expectations, however, drove me into quicker action in the hope Billy had something, anything, to help me weave together these dangling loose ends I had.

The rain increased its pace, hitting the windshield in sheets, like some invisible rain-man was throwing buckets of water at me from a springboard on the bumper of my car. My pessimistic side was convinced it always rained harder when I was obliged to be outside.

I drove around the bay and down to the parking lot adjacent to the beach, put on the warm jacket and wool hat, and braced myself for what I knew wouldn't be a leisurely shoreline stroll. It was even colder next to the ocean, and a stiff breeze further chilled the air, blasting ice-cold moisture against my face. I turned up my collar and trudged along, head down to fight off the wet wind, looking up occasionally for signs of life.

Big River Beach is only about 500 yards long and half that wide, nestled at the far end of the bay, surrounded by a semicircle of tall cliffs. When the tide goes out, the beach increases in size, but today it was in and relatively high. On a nice day, several groups of locals and tourists would be playing volleyball with makeshift nets, or sitting around driftwood campfires, roasting hot dogs and marshmallows. Weather conditions today, however, kept those with any sense from venturing out, except for one couple walking hand in hand along the water's edge in the wake of a big red dog that played keep-away with the waves and barked at the crashing surf.

There was no sign of Billy Spencer. I thought the least I could do after making this gallant effort was to approach the couple.

"Hi, I was supposed to meet a friend down here about an hour ago and I was wondering if you might have seen him."

"We thought we were the only ones foolish enough to come out today," the man answered, pulling up his collar even tighter around his face to block the persistent pelting rain.

"Has there been anyone else down here?" I asked, holding my arms around myself to try to contain what little body heat I had left.

"Haven't seen anyone on the beach, and we've been here about half an hour, maybe forty-five minutes. Had to give our dog a workout—he was driving us crazy holed up in the hotel room. There was a guy in the parking lot, though, leaving just as we pulled in."

"Was he a young skinny guy?"

"No, an older man, maybe fifty or sixty. I didn't get a good look at him. He drove off in a black BMW, if that's any help," he offered.

"I may want to talk with you some more," I said, the downpour making it somewhat difficult to give him one of my business cards: my hands were so wet and cold that it was an effort to bend my fingers and reach into my pocket for it. The man handed me a card of his own. He was a computer something-or-other from San Francisco. I thanked them both and raced for my Volvo and shelter from the wet, biting cold.

As soon as I set foot in my office, I stripped off my soaked outer garments and stood by the wall heater for ten minutes, long enough to give my blood a chance to thaw and begin circulating. I was disappointed to have missed Billy. From what I'd gathered, he didn't have the stamina to wait very long in the cold. I couldn't blame him, but I was curious as hell why he had bothered to contact me. Something had to have changed his earlier attitude.

The answering machine's red eye winked at me. Hoping it was Billy, I pressed the button; it was a woman answering my ad. I dialed her number immediately.

"Why, hello, dear, this is Mrs. Covington."

"Oh, are you Sally Covington, the artist?"

"Yes, I suppose you could call me that. I dabble some," she said in a warm, friendly tone.

I'd seen some of her work in a local art show, and often read about her in the paper, because she's a leading political activist on the coast. A crusty old eccentric, she's lived in the area close to fifty years, and when she isn't painting seascapes in watercolors, she's seated in the Mendocino County Board of Supervisors' chambers, fighting for one cause or another. Even though she looks like the classic grandmother central casting would send out with warm cookies and a pitcher of milk, she possesses a sharp tongue and fights as fiercely as a pit bull about anything she strongly supports or, in most cases, opposes.

Sally is a staunch believer in, if not the leader of, the anti-development movement in Mendocino. It pains her, as it does many other old-timers, to see rapid growth taking place with little regard for overall planning, and its impact on the quiet nature of the picturesque village. A shortage of water, since all properties are on tenuous wells, and the eventual lack of sufficient parking spaces are two paramount issues. Every time someone opens a new restaurant where formerly a single-family dwelling existed, or converts a private residence into a bed and breakfast inn, water usage escalates. City visitors aren't accustomed to water conservation consciousness. Some businesses concerned with the dilemma have posted signs that say, to the vacationers' puzzlement, FLUSH ONLY WHEN NECESSARY or, IF IT'S YELLOW, LET IT MELLOW; IF IT'S BROWN, FLUSH IT DOWN.

Sally serves on the stringent Mendocino Historical Review Board, which tries, sometimes fruitlessly, to curb development in the village, but is slowly being limited to exterior architectural style issues and sign permits, by big-time developers with tons of money and political clout, who regularly take their appeals to the board of supervisors to get the review board's denial of their expansive projects overturned. Since the village is unincorporated, there's no town council, so it's at the mercy of Mendocino County officials who savor the revenues the village's development brings in.

I suspected Sally would eventually steer the conversation to her current political battle. I support a lot of her beliefs, especially a slower pace on new development, but at the same time I sympathize with small merchants like Lucia, whose livelihoods depend on the tourist industry. I'm opposed to huge new structures that are out of proportion to existing buildings and block the ocean views of neighboring homes that have existed since the turn of the century. It seems unfair. Also, every time a new well is drilled in town, it pulls water from everyone else's well, just like a new straw added to a communal milkshake, since all the water comes from the same aquifer. Sooner or later, a municipal water system would have to be installed.

"I admire your work, Mrs. Covington, both artistically and politically. You're excellent on both counts."

"Thank you. I've been at it a long time, and there's always more to do each day, as I'm sure you're aware. You've heard what they want to do with the new post office, haven't you?"

"Oh, yes." I wanted to listen, but steered the conversation back to my business instead, feeling a bit impatient. "You mentioned you were responding to my ad. What did you see?"

"Well, I was driving up Little Lake Road last Saturday to visit my friend, Mrs. Murray. She hasn't been feeling too well, so I was taking her some soup I made the night before. She lives about four and a half miles up the road."

"Uh-huh."

"I don't know exactly where I was, but before I got to her house, I saw one of those armored trucks driving ahead of me. I know I saw it, because it reminded me I had forgotten to go the bank to use that new machine they have now, and take out some cash to bring to Mrs. Murray, so she could pay for a load of firewood she was having delivered. The man wouldn't take a check. He insisted on cash; you know, doesn't want to pay taxes. What do you call it? Under the table, or something like that."

I wanted to fast-forward her but didn't know how to do it without being rude.

"For a minute," she continued, "when I saw the truck, I thought maybe Mrs. Murray asked the bank to deliver the money to her, but Lord, it was only a hundred dollars, and I didn't think they would make such a big fuss over it. Anyway, I had to turn around and go all the way back to the village just to get the money I had forgotten."

"Did you see the truck again when you went back up the road?"

"No, but it was quite awhile before I went back up, because I met Margo at the bank and we got to talking, and you know how that is. We're like a couple of old hens, we just carry on for the longest time."

"Okay, Mrs. Covington. Thank you. You've been a great help." I sensed our conversation, or rather her running monologue, would go on forever if I didn't close it soon.

"Strange, that truck being out there," she added, just as I was about to hang up. "Don't know where it was headed. There sure aren't any banks up that road. It just dead ends eight miles ahead at the children's camp."

CHAPTER 7

Frank Spencer was listed in the new phone book that had been dropped off, wrapped in clear plastic, at the end of my driveway just last week. The phone company doesn't believe in delivering to the doorsteps in the countryside. Ma Bell may say otherwise, but I believe the reason she won't personally hand the new book over or drop it at the front door is due to the "big dog factor," an issue well known and taken into account by pollsters like Gallup.

Since most residents in this country are more likely to cooperate if a pollster is female, more pollsters employ female interviewers. If said female walks up to a home with the lights on, maybe a television blaring in the background, but a big dog approaches, hunger in its menacing eyes, the interviewer, paid little more than minimum wage, has to ask herself if she's going to risk life and limb for the interview. Nine times out of ten she'll check the box on her questionnaire indicating, "Not at home." Thus owners of big dogs are rarely accounted for in random samples taken of the general population in any door-to-door survey, and phone directories aren't hand delivered in dog-infested rural areas.

I dialed Spencer's number, giving it a full ten rings with no answer from Billy or anyone else, before I hung up and dialed

Anne's number; no answer at the Phelps residence either. I was beginning to wonder why, despite her father's proclamation, Anne hadn't been in touch with me, even if she was out of town. She was too troubled not to be interested in my investigation and its eventual conclusions, even if the case presently had more loose ends than an industrial-size rag mop.

It was five o'clock, already getting dark, and the rain continued pouring down, its incessant cadence hitting my roof like a troupe of beginning tap dancers having a marathon rehearsal overhead. The notion of going home to a bowl of cold cereal wasn't exceedingly appealing, so I drove over to the Seagull Inn for a bowl of warm clam chowder. Despite Lucia's criticism of the chowder, for the first time all day I felt comforted. Hot chocolate was the only other thing on the menu capable of doing the job, but I was trying to be health conscious for a few minutes.

Just as I was finishing my chowder and debating whether to have a piece of warm pumpkin pie with a scoop of vanilla ice cream on top, in strolled Sally Covington. My first reaction was to hide under the table. Since our earlier conversation, I'd had an uncanny feeling Sally was going to hunt me down to assist her in whatever political cause she was championing this week. I'd managed to avoid all her issues during our phone conversation, but knew Sally was a persistent, unyielding character.

Somewhat timidly, yet with a firm look on her pink and wrinkled face, she stood over my table, her arms burdened with bundles of file folders and newspapers. Without asking, she plopped herself down across from me, deposited her papers on the tabletop, and whispered, "You're a detective, aren't you?"

What could I say? "Yes, I am."

"It wasn't until after our talk that I put your name, face, and occupation together. I could certainly use your help, and there is no time to waste. This is an urgent matter," she said, that innocent, grandmotherly face now serious.

Not wanting to encourage her, I said, "Well, I'm right in the middle of a pretty big case right now, and can't really take on another one yet."

She raised her eyebrows, looking disappointed and shocked at the same time, but nevertheless carried on: "But this will only take a few minutes of your time. Surely you understand."

The waitress came over and asked Sally if she wanted anything. Sally brushed her away as though the last reason she might enter a restaurant would be to order anything to eat. In part from compassion for the waitress, but mostly due to my lingering sweet tooth, I ordered the pumpkin pie.

"O.K., Sally, what's on your mind?" I said, trying to sound enthusiastic.

She sighed heavily and settled more comfortably into her chair. "There is this developer in the village. He owns a lot of property and is building two new structures. Although he managed to finagle his way through the building department and board of supervisors to get permits for his latest skyscraper, I know he's cheating and doing things he doesn't have permits for," she announced, accenting the word "skyscraper" as if it were a highly poisonous insect crawling up my neck.

Sensing I was going to get a lengthy history of this man, and hoping to forestall it, I said, "Where do I come into the scheme of things?"

"I just want you to walk with me down to the buildings to investigate a few things. It'll be pitch black in another few minutes; all the shops will be closed and their owners home for the evening, so no one will see us snooping around," she said, a gleam in her eye. I had to hand it to her, she was irresistible; I felt like she was my grandma, asking me to prepare a cup of tea and straighten the bed covers for her. How could I refuse this kindly, eccentric, and determined woman?

"I suppose you want to do this tonight. It can't wait?" I asked, looking into her intense eyes, which were eroding my last bank of resistance.

"Yes. You see, the board of supervisors meets tomorrow and I must have this information by nine tomorrow morning."

My pie arrived and I slowly savored the combination of warm pumpkin flavor and cool vanilla ice cream. I suspected every time I indulged in one of these calorically decadent desserts that it would take several days at the health club to work it off. I continued rationalizing through the entire consumption of my pie, with thoughts like *I deserve this because I'm going to help this sweet old lady* — my way of devising plausible excuses for my desires, despite being fully aware of my real motive, which revolved around my taste buds.

Sally watched me, a little impatient with my slow eating. I reached into my purse and drew out enough money for the meal and tip, leaving both on the table with the check, and looked up at Sally. "O.K., let's go," I announced.

She picked up all her papers and we headed out to her beat-up car, parallel parked behind mine in front of the restaurant. *The old coot followed me from my office, I bet.* She motioned for me to get in the passenger side, which was stacked high with additional papers and file folders. I tossed them in the backseat and sat down, straddling even more files and newspapers heaped on the floorboards. Sally backed up, hitting the car behind her, and then nicked my rear bumper as she turned the wheel to pull out of the parking place. I was grateful we weren't going on an extended drive. She flipped a U-turn and headed back west toward the center of town.

This time avoiding neighboring bumpers — easy, since the village was virtually deserted — Sally parked in an alley parallel to the street we were headed for. She asked me to grab a brown duffel bag out of the backseat to take along with us. It was heavy. I didn't ask what it contained. Matching her determined stride, I followed alongside her, wondering just what the hell I was getting myself into. We were approaching a building, enormous by Mendocino standards, still under construction. I could see the exterior plywood and tarpaper in place, but the horizontal clapboard siding was only half completed on the one-story structure, which featured exceptionally high ceilings and an attic space with dormers on both the east and west sides. The rain had subsided, but it was cold; I pulled my collar up.

"Now, here's what I suspect," Sally whispered, close to my ear. "This guy had permits for a one-story structure with attic space above it for storage. He is limited to small water usage because the wells in this part of the village can't sustain any more drilling. He is going to rent it out for retail shops that don't require water except for one toilet. What I think he's doing is preparing to convert that attic area into an apartment with additional toilets, bathtubs, kitchen sinks, the whole works."

"So what do you propose we do?" I asked.

She fumbled around in the duffel bag I had put down where we stood behind the building, and pulled out a claw hammer. "First, we have to pry off a piece of this plywood and get inside," she said, as matter-of-factly as if discussing how to spread the frosting on a birthday cake.

None of the windows or doors had been installed yet, so all the openings were temporarily sealed with half-inch plywood tacked in place with sixpenny nails driven about three-fourths of the way in, so the carpenters could easily remove them to gain access—and so could we. I chose a door in the back, where it was darker and less visible from the street, and pried the nails out while Sally stood watch. Once inside, I propped the plywood back in place against the jams, so anyone who might chance to pass by wouldn't encounter a gaping hole. Sally produced a flashlight, and we made our way slowly and carefully over piles of sheetrock and lumber, to a makeshift ladder to the attic area.

"Are you sure you want to go up there with me? I can just look around and report back to you," I said, realizing we'd have a lot of explaining to do if we got caught, and could both be arrested for breaking and entering. I sensed it didn't faze Sally a bit. Maybe when you get older you don't give a shit about little things like B & E's, or being arrested, handcuffed, fingerprinted, and kept in a holding cell that reeked of urine and vomit, until a bondsman came to your rescue. Sally must be seventy-five, hardly an age for climbing ladders, or so I thought.

"You bet I am," Sally answered. "This is the best part. You don't think for a minute, young lady, that you're going to leave me down here?"

So much for that. I decided to let Sally ascend the ladder first; if she lost her balance I could make some attempt to catch her or at least break her fall. Once up top, I was thankful to see the sub-floor was down, and we wouldn't be balancing ourselves on joists with gaps wide enough for us to fall to our deaths. Sally flashed the light around until she saw what she was looking for.

"See? Over there. I told you," she said. We walked over to the area she was pointing to with her flashlight. Between the studs in the exposed framing, we could see plumbing pipes snaking through from the first floor: both hot and cold copper pipe inlets led to two separate areas in this part of the attic; black plastic ABS sewer pipes in three more locations joined a common, wider ABS pipe leading back down to the first floor.

In another section of the attic we found more copper pipes, indicating additional hot and cold inlets, as well as ABS sewer pipes. We both concluded the attic was plumbed for a bathroom as well as a kitchen.

"None of this is in the building plans," Sally hissed. "When the inspector comes by they probably cover it all up with plywood."

"We've seen what you were looking for, so let's get the hell out of here," I suggested.

We went back down the ladder, gingerly walked over the building materials, nailed the plywood back in place as quietly as one can hammer in the still of the night, and sauntered back over to Sally's car like two cats with juicy mice in our mouths.

"You can just drive me back to my car now," I said, grateful to have this little escapade over with.

"Oh, there's one more little thing I need help with," she said. "This won't take as long, either. There's another building on the other end of the village that's finished. The owner was limited to a certain height, and I'm sure it's taller that the plans called for. Do you mind?"

Of course I minded, but that wasn't the point. I'd already gone this far, might as well give her a few more minutes of my time, even though I had no intention of charging her for my services. It was the least I could do for her cause.

"No, I'm in. Let's go," I said, as cheerfully as I could. What I really wanted to do was go home and crawl into bed with a good book.

Turning the car around once again, she headed back in the direction we had come from, and stopped farther up the same alley in the next block. This time she extracted a huge tape measure from her glove box. We walked down the alley to another street running north of it. A new two-story building, one of the largest in the village, was our destination. Construction was complete, but the painters were still working on the final coat. They had left their scaffolding in place, as well as a number of extension ladders. Thievery is never of serious concern in the village, so builders tend to leave more equipment around building sites than they would in the city.

"I'm pretty feisty, as you've probably noticed, but my sea legs aren't what they used to be. I need to have you crawl up on the roof with the tape, hold it at the peak, and throw the other end down to me so I can see just exactly how high this thing is," she announced, again as if it were an everyday task, no more difficult than decorating the cake we had just frosted.

All I have to do is crawl up on the roof of a two-story building.

No big deal, Sally. Of course it's no big deal to *her*, for crying out loud, because she gets to stay on the ground. Speechless, I took the cloth tape measure from her hand, shook my head in disbelief, and began climbing the scaffold to the edge of the roof. I never considered myself a second-story woman, and was beginning to feel like I'd been thrust into a bizarre time warp, with Agatha Christie's Miss Marple guiding me through one of her adventures. At the same time, I wasn't exactly enamored of heights, and knew that looking down would send waves of fear through my body, so I forced my eyes upward and tried to think of anything besides where I was. Thank God it had stopped raining, and my tennis shoes still had plenty of tread for gripping the slippery wet surfaces.

The roofers had secured some two-by-fours to the steeply pitched roof to enable the chimney installer to reach his destination. I used these to get to the peak, which amounted to perching myself about three stories up. Sally looked on from below, waiting patiently for me to throw down the heavy body of the tape, a circular affair with a lock on its side, which brought back memories of my father, who had a similar tape measure in a handsome leather case. I said a quick prayer for him in his eternal home in the afterlife—and for my safe return to the Mendocino soil below.

Lying flat on my stomach, I held my end firmly at the highest point of the roof peak, and dropped the tape down to Sally. She pulled it taunt, nodded, and gave a little wave for me to release it. Satisfied my job was completed, I cautiously made a slow descent along the makeshift steps to the scaffold and finally back down to terra firma.

"It's just like I thought: it's a good eight feet taller than the plans called for. That's why I keep insisting they ask for models made to scale of all the buildings in the village. Then people can visualize what these monstrosities are going to look like before they go up," she said bitterly.

When we were getting back into Sally's car, I noticed a dark sedan parked at the end of the street. From where we were parked I couldn't make out the figure behind the wheel. As Sally made her way back down the street, I tried to see inside the car, but it was very dark and that section of the village had no streetlights. The shadow looked a little like Templeton the rat, but I couldn't be sure. The car was a late-model BMW.

After Sally dropped me at my car, thanking me profusely for the help, I drove back to where the rat had been parked. The car was gone. As a precaution, I took a roundabout route back to my cabin to be certain I wasn't being followed.

Once inside, I started a fire, took a long warm shower, fed the Tank—all in reverse order, naturally, since Tank has the patience and understanding of a meter maid—and then curled up in bed with a new book. I was asleep before I finished the first chapter.

CHAPTER 8

When I awoke about nine thirty the next morning, later than usual, sunshine greeted me, pouring through the south window and splashing across my down comforter. My sleuthing antics with Mendocino's Miss Marple, out to save the village from pillage and plunder last night, combined with my frigid trek on the beach earlier, had been enough exertion to push my automatic sleep meter into overtime. I stretched and rolled over, debating whether to spend a few more hours in a cozy horizontal position or get up and face another day of detecting.

At the foot of my bed, Tank lay sleeping on top of the television—a thirteen-incher much too small to contain his enormous bulk, which hung over all four sides of it. At least once a week, deep in cat slumber, he'll move his head a little too far to one side and its weight will topple his corpulent mid-section onto the floor. He covers this clumsy act with feline nonchalance, usually a bathing maneuver, as if he'd intended all along to do a back flip off the TV.

I put coffee water on, and looked out the south window; the sun continued to stream in. I was pleased not to have to defend myself again from the moister elements of life in the northwest. Some cumulus clouds in the western sky looked like giant cream puffs. Innocent and delicious as they appeared, I dressed in warm clothing and took my raincoat from its hook, placing it next to my purse by the front door to remind myself not to be fooled, as the weather here can change quicker than Steve Young could hand off to Garrison Hearst when Steve was the 49ers' star quarterback.

Since I was leaving for the office, I poured my coffee into a thermos to drink on the way into the village, and grabbed a granola bar to tide me over till lunch. Hearing me fussing in the kitchen, Tank came in for his breakfast and a short visit before I dashed out the door.

As it turned out, Lucia was late for work too, and just putting up her open sign when I pulled up in front of the shop. I walked over to her.

"Hi Syracuse. Still hot on someone's trail? I've missed you since our little dinner date the other night," she said, a soft lilt in her voice. I suspected she wanted something.

"I wish I were. I'm working on a jigsaw puzzle that doesn't have enough pieces to outline the shape yet. It's frustrating as hell," I said.

"Well, your buddy Ed was by a few minutes ago looking for you. Maybe he's got some of the outer edges in his toy box."

"Oh? What'd he say?"

"To call him as soon as you get in."

"Great. Thanks, I'll go do that." I started to leave, but Lucia put her hand on my arm.

"Before you run off with Wyatt Earp, do me a little favor and help me string these Christmas lights around the front windows. It'll only take a second."

Remembering the little favor I'd been asked to do the night before, I was beginning to feel like the village handyman, or perhaps the village idiot.

"Sure," I found myself saying. "You wouldn't believe what Sally Covington got me into last night. She literally had me crawling around rooftops with her, gathering ammunition to take to the board of supervisors today. She's pissed at some developer and she's going to read him the riot act today in her own unremitting fashion. She's such a great old character. Do you know her?"

"Who doesn't? Occasionally she stops in, asking us to sign one petition or another to stop this or start that. I heard her house is filled floor to ceiling with newspapers and handwritten notes on legal pads."

"Yeah. Her car holds what doesn't fit in the house," I added.

Lucia walked back to the storeroom and brought out a cardboard box with "Christmas Decorations" scrawled on its side. She plopped it down on the floor at my feet. We spent the next half hour tangled up in green cords and clear lights, finally figuring out a foolproof system before we'd reached the last window, Lucia unreeling the cords as I push-pinned them around the trim at six-inch intervals, careful not to stab the delicate wires and electrocute myself. As a private detective, my life comes into danger more frequently than it would in other occupations. I'd rather "go out" gallantly, as opposed to foolishly or carelessly. Putting up Christmas lights is not my way of going.

"That does it, kiddo, I'm outta here," I said, after plunging the final pin.

"Stop by tonight and see how pretty they look when it begins to get dark."

"Gotta run now," I answered.

"Off to leap more tall buildings in a single bound?" Lucia giggled.

"Something like that," I said, heading out the door.

It was eleven o'clock when I sat down at my desk. There were several messages on the machine: Ed had called twice, both times to say it was extremely important to call him. Two simultaneous thoughts crossed my mind: either he was stoned again or he had some news about my armored truck. I said a brief silent prayer for the latter.

Sally Covington had called from Ukiah with an update on what the board of supervisors thought of our evening's caper. She said she'd call me when she got back home, but just wanted me to know things were going in our favor and lots of heads were presently rolling.

I poured the last of the coffee from the thermos, dialed Ed's number, and leaned back in my swivel chair.

"Nelson here," he answered.

"What's goin' on Ed?"

"I should ask you. Where the hell have you been?"

"Slept in. Had a rough night."

"Remember that client of yours who reported the possible truck heist?"

"Of course I do, Ed, that was just a few days ago. I still have plenty of brain cells left and they're functioning quite well, thank you."

"Sorry, Syracuse, but I'd sort of put her out of my mind, Anyway, she's the daughter of Frank Spencer—you know, the president of the Bank of Mendocino."

"I know that, too. Why don't you get to the point?" I said, a little irritated because I was hungry, my blood sugar dropping to dangerous levels.

"She's got a kid brother named Billy."

"I'm afraid that's three strikes Ed. You're not telling me anything I don't already know."

"Try this curveball. His body washed up on Big River Beach this morning, discovered by two tourists who probably won't vacation here again next year."

"Shit. What happened?" I exclaimed.

"Finally threw a pitch you liked, huh? Coroner's with him now; preliminary's probably drowning."

"Drowning? How the hell can anybody drown at Big River Beach? No one even swims there, the water's too cold," I said, my voice a bit more hysterical than I was comfortable with. I'd also bet my last Snicker's bar that Billy hadn't been swimming in the rain, either.

"Beats me. The family hasn't been notified yet, so keep it under your hat, at least until you hear back from me."

When will Corry have the results of the final?" Corry was Dr. Howard Corry, the local coroner, a jolly, pudgy guy, never short of quick one-liners, who maintained his sanity in a gruesome occupation by being able to laugh at his plight—unlike undertakers, who keep their composed, reserved demeanors on exhibit, as if death must always be a serious matter.

"Probably not until tomorrow," Ed answered.

"Okay. I'll drop by late afternoon and talk to him. Thanks a lot, Ed."

Shit. I didn't want to tell Ed I was supposed to meet Billy at the beach, not yet anyway, not until I could digest this startling news. All my instincts told me something besides salmon and cod was fishy on that beach. Unfortunately whatever "fucking important" thing Billy wanted to talk to me about was lost forever in the cold waters of Big River Bay.

Deciding that some fresh air might clear the cobwebs out of my brain, I walked downstairs and around the corner to the Chocolate Moose for lunch. The sky was blue, but still held enormous white clouds, followed farther out to sea by a blanket of gray fog destined to reach the shore within an hour. Although it was sunny and warm, as soon as the fog hit, the temperature would drop several degrees. In preparation, I had a bowl of cream of potato soup with a miniature loaf of French bread, virtuously skipping dessert.

I spent the rest of the afternoon lying to receptionists at various hospitals throughout the county, trying to track down which one Spencer's wife was incarcerated in. Mildred, the bank teller, provided me her first name, Elizabeth, but didn't know which institution she was in, only that it was out of town. Of the three neighboring counties, I finally hit pay dirt in Sonoma County, to the south. Elizabeth Spencer was in a small private hospital in Santa Rosa, about two hours' drive from Mendocino. I told the receptionist, as I had all the others, that Elizabeth Spencer was my aunt and I would like to speak with her. To ask whether she was a patient there would have been a dead giveaway, so I approached each hospital as if certain she was—just one of those little white lies that leave the tiniest of impressions on the soul, half a prayer's worth of indulgence for full forgiveness.

"She is not able to accept calls right now," was all the information I needed and got from the curt secretary in Santa Rosa to assure me I'd scored. Sometimes I try to squeeze out more details in a situation like this, but I intuited that it would be safer at this point to take the information I'd got and hang up before the receptionist had an opportunity to ask me any questions.

My previous career as an investigative reporter was excellent training for conducting interviews as a detective. Occasionally, I identify myself as a reporter if I think it will make things flow more smoothly. Sometimes, people are so flattered to talk to a reporter that they become overly generous with any information they have, but in this case, it was much better to be the concerned niece.

That methodical and conventional bit of detecting accomplished, I traced Frank Spencer's previous employment to a bank in Orange County. Assuming Billy lived with his old man in Los Angeles, I checked police records there through a friend of Ed's in the department who had access to the computer files. Picked up for possession of marijuana and possession with intent to sell; the charges were dropped both times, undoubtedly because Spencer could afford to hire a fancy lawyer capable of playing the loopholes in the criminal justice system.

After moving to Mendocino with the rest of the clan about six months ago, Billy's activities along the coastline had been subdued, at least as far as I could ascertain until I had a chance to check with some of my street sources. Gainful employment wasn't exactly etched in Billy's forehead; it was apparent he received his basic needs, food, clothing, and shelter, from his father, but relied on the seamy side of life for his nastier interests.

I typed up all my notes on the case to date, vowing that as long as there were threads to unravel, I'd continue to move onward and sideways through the fabric.

It was five-thirty. I turned off my desk lamp, walked out the door and down the stairs to Lucia's store. It was foggy and cold; I buttoned up my jacket and stepped into the shop.

"Want to have an official lighting ceremony?" I asked.

"I was just getting ready to do that," Lucia said, as she bent over to plug the array of cords into a quadruple outlet box behind the faux-granite counter. Suddenly, the clothes in the window displays were bathed in the artificial glow of the tiny Christmas lights.

"Not too shabby a job for Superwoman," I said proudly.

"C'mon. Let's see if we can find you some kryptonite for dinner," she laughed, and we headed out to the street.

CHAPTER 9

In Mendocino the coroner works out of the sheriff's department, so Howard Corry's office is part of the log cabin Western scene where Ed is stationed. I strolled in the familiar front door the next afternoon, just as Corry, his back to me, was handing Ed a thin manila file folder. I recognized Corry immediately by his bald spot, a near-perfect circle surrounded by jet-black wavy hair. It always reminded me of the visiting Catholic monks who taught theology at the all girls' Catholic high school I attended in the late 1950s. As a teenager, I assumed all these monks went to the same barber and gave up their hair for Jesus or the Holy Ghost.

Corry was far from spiritual material, however, and had taken to wearing hats much of the time when he was outside the office in an effort to conceal what he thought was the loss of his manhood hair by hair—the one subject he didn't joke about.

"Well, if it isn't the lady dick. What's up, Syracuse?" Corry bellowed as I approached the front desk.

"Very funny, Howard. I'd like to talk to you for a minute about the Spencer kid."

"Sure. Excuse us, Ed, be back in a bit to go over the rest of this with you," Corry said, as he pointed me in the direction of his office at the rear of the building.

Corry's private domain always gives me the creeps, since more often than not, various body parts can be found resting on huge, plastic-covered worktables at the far end of the small office and laboratory he operates in. I crept in the door slowly, took a quick look around to be certain no eerie and repulsive specimens might startle me in mid-sentence, and then sat on one of the tall stools Corry used so he could lean close to his wretched, slimy specimens of flesh, bone, and blood. Shit, it's no wonder he maintains a state of high humor—what a hideous job absent a lighthearted attitude.

"What did you want to know?" Corry asked as soon as we were seated.

"What killed the kid?"

"Heroin overdose."

"What?" I said, not trusting I'd heard him correctly.

"You heard me right. Billy Spencer died of a heroin overdose."

I paused, then asked, "What can you tell me about it?"

"Only that it was a potent one, enough to kill a horse or two," he cackled.

"Can you tell if it was self-inflicted?"

"They usually are. No way of knowing for sure, though, if you mean did somebody pop him. There was only one needle mark, perfectly placed in the vein on his forearm, so I'd say he wasn't a regular user, or there would've been tracks up and down his arms like a hiker's map of Yosemite," Corry chuckled. "He might not have known how much to do, is my guess, and he just accidentally overdid his first, and I might add, last, time out."

"Any other marks on the body?"

"Nothing out of the ordinary."

Puzzled, I asked, "How do you suppose he wound up in the water?"

"I can only guess. He might have shot up on the beach and

then walked a few feet into the surf before the OD hit. It killed him almost instantly, so he would have fallen headfirst into the drink. There wasn't any water in his lungs, so he was dead before he was submerged. What's your interest, Syracuse?" he inquired.

"His sister is a client of mine. Damn it, Howard, I might as well come clean now, since I will sooner or later. I met Billy a few days ago when I was working on a case. He left word on my answering machine day before yesterday to meet him at Big River Beach at noon. I didn't get the message until almost one, and he was gone by the time I got there," I grumbled.

"Gone in more ways than one, I'd say. Time of death was closer to noon. Looks like you were stood up," he laughed.

"Is this going down as accidental?" I said, trying to get some idea how the department was going to handle it.

"For now, unless new evidence comes in to the contrary."

"Thanks Howard. I better go tell Ed what I just told you, and see what the department wants to do with this."

I walked back up the long corridor to the front office, weighing the idea that Billy had to have been murdered. Why in hell would he call me to meet him if he was going to kill himself before I got there, or try to get so loaded that he'd be inarticulate? It didn't make any sense, but neither did a lot of things in my line of work.

It was nice to see the old sparkle in Ed's hazel eyes again, the shine previously buried behind the bloodshot barriers of a few days ago. Ed was reading a report when I walked over to his desk. I told him about my ill-fated appointment with Billy. He stared at me questioningly and said, "I suppose you think he was offed?"

"I don't want to rule out that possibility yet," I answered. I knew Ed could see I was noticeably upset over this afternoon's turn of events. He dropped his businesslike demeanor, and concern spread across his face, like I'd just been thrown out at first on a lousy call from a cold-hearted umpire.

"I get off in ten minutes. Want to go out for some coffee and talk it over?"

Jocks, former or present, always surprise me when they let the sweeter side of their personalities show through their tight, muscular bodies. Ed was no exception. I was cautious with him, though, because I'd learned over the years he was one of those "When he was good, he was very, very good, and when he was bad, he was horrid" types. We'd gotten closer the past few days, as we had so many times before, and though I appreciated and enjoyed Ed's attention, I was guarded when I felt my heart opening to him again. I felt like I was inviting the kind Dr. Jekyll into my home, knowing full well he was capable of turning into the vicious Dr. Hyde before I had time to close the door. Emotional pain from this department of the sheriff's office wasn't anything I craved in life.

My schizophrenic mood responded, echoing my confusion. "Sure. Why don't we drive into Fort Bragg and have dinner at the harbor. I could sure use the company," I said, throwing every ounce of caution to the proverbial wind, "and Tank would love the leftovers."

"Great idea. I just have to finish up with Howard. It'll only take a few minutes. My truck's parked out back, if you want to pull your rig around and meet me in the lot," he smiled.

"Fine. I'll wait for you back there."

I walked out the heavy door, down the wooden steps, past the hitching posts and rail full of imaginary horses, and visualized them looking like they'd been ridden hard and put up wet, milky sweat dripping from their brown hides, by sheriffs of yesteryear. I drove around back and parked next to Ed's red pickup. Although muddled ideas spun in my head, my mind like an out-of-control milkshake mixer waiting for its contents to settle, I felt the way I do when I step up to a poker slot machine in Reno: like there was a lot more at stake now than a real or imagined armored truck, and my gambler's instincts went for broke. I could feel the adrenalin entering my blood, the growing excitement, the thrill of hitting the big jackpot.

This was the point in a new case where I knew there was no turning back. I was firmly hooked and willing to be reeled in. Finding Anne was crucial. There'd been no answer at her house all day. Although I dreaded another encounter with Spencer, I decided to drive out to Anne's in the morning.

I hungered for more information about heroin. Corry had been helpful, but I needed to know more. My best source for the facts, especially here on the coast, would be the man who heads up the substance-abuse program in Fort Bragg, Richard Powers, at the public health department's county offices.

I pulled down the visor in my Volvo to reveal a mirror, straightened my hair, applied mascara, and studied my features, a miniscule moment of vanity before Ed stepped out the back door. I got out of my car, locked it, and entered his truck.

The drive up the coast to Fort Bragg took us ten minutes. Traffic was light and there wasn't a single slow-moving log truck making its way to the lumber mill on Main Street. Fort Bragg was Small Town, USA, population about 5,000, many of them employed by the logging companies or in the fishing industry. Behind the colorful history of logging camps, backwoods distilleries during Prohibition, and the Biblical fishing industry, are hardworking families whose fourth- and fifth-generation descendants still live and work on the coast.

Neighbors chat with one another over backyard fences, kids are within walking distance of their schools, and Bingo is the biggest game in town, played every other night at either the Catholic Church or one of the service clubs. Funeral notices are still posted on two light-poles at downtown locations.

The largest fishing port between San Francisco and Eureka is in Fort Bragg: the Noyo River harbor, where we were headed for dinner. It's a working port with a fleet of commercial fishing boats that harvest salmon, snapper, cod, crab, and sea urchins.

Snapper was the only kind of fish I ever ate, except for the occasional salmon fillet at one of the barbecues the coast is noted for. Fort Bragg boasts "The world's largest salmon barbecue," held every Fourth of July.

Ed turned onto Harbor Drive leading to the port below. The steep, twisting road hugged the cliffs down to the mouth of the river, the commercial docks, fish-cleaning buildings, tackle shops, motels, and restaurants. It was the perfect time to be at the harbor, early evening, when all the fishing boats line up one by one and slowly make their way into the narrow estuary. Fishing seemed such a romantic occupation when viewed from the shoreline.

Ed and I were quiet during the drive from Mendocino, but once seated at a window table overlooking the docks, we got down to business immediately.

"Are you keeping something from me, Syracuse? I get the impression there's more going on here than you've told me or the department about, and if my boss starts getting suspicious he's going to haul you in for questioning."

Blessed with the same tall, dark, and handsome features of any current leading man, Ed was truly a gorgeous individual. Despite the serious allegation he had just brought up, I caught myself daydreaming about what a hunk he was. Looking into his clear, bright eyes, I said, "I've told you all there is to tell. You know that Anne came to my office with her truck story, and that I met Billy at Anne's house. He called me the next day and wanted to meet me at the beach, but took a permanent powder instead."

When a waitress came to our table, we both ordered coffee for starters, and fish-and-chips dinners. Her bleached blonde hair and incessant gum snapping reminded me of a Walgreen's lunch counter character from the 1950s. We were not in a classy dive, but the food is cheap and good, and the view is one of only a few ocean vistas from any of the coastal eateries.

"There's got to be more, Syracuse. I know you too well; you wouldn't be so immersed in this case if there weren't. If you didn't have more to go on, you'd blow this off," Ed said.

"O.K., there are a couple of other minor details. Anne's father, an asshole in my opinion, came by my office and ordered me to drop the investigation. He claimed Anne was cuckoo and my work with her was too stressful for her delicate condition."

"Uh-huh. Anything else?"

"She retained me, and I don't like this guy pushing me around. I'm doing it for spite now—continuing on the case, I mean."

"Anything else, Syracuse?" Ed asked, grinning softly, as though he could read my mind and knew I was still withholding.

"Anything else," I repeated. "Well, I did check with Harriet Ross, and she verified there'd been no use of an armored truck up here for movies or commercials, so I still don't know why Anne insists she saw one, except I do have another witness who saw the truck a little earlier that day on the same road, and I did find a tiny clue at the scene of the alleged crime. Too minor to bother mentioning," I added teasingly.

"Yeah. Like what kind of tiny clue?"

"What will you give me if I tell you?" I answered brazenly.

"How about a date to the Giants' exposition game against the A's?"

"You really know the way to a girl's heart, even one who prides herself on her confidentiality clause. O.K., I give. I found a cap, a guard's cap. That must mean something happened out there. It can't be some weird coincidence."

"Hmm. That *is* kind of intriguing. Now I see why you're sticking with this. You probably think the reason Billy tried to reach you is because he knew something about it, and knowing you, you took it one step further and assumed he was killed to keep him from singing."

"That sums it up nicely, but I'd like to continue on my own for a while; see what else I can uncover before I ask the Department to step in. Can you keep it quiet just a little longer?"

"Sure," he said, without a moment's hesitation.

Our food arrived, and after eating and two more hours of meaningful conversation, drifting from detecting to flirting with one another, we wound up back at Ed's old Victorian in Mendocino, stretched out in front of the fireplace, watching the flames flicker in tune with our inner heat. The chemistry between us was undeniable and irresistible. I blamed a lot of the attraction tonight on ovulation, forcing me to allow my desires to rule my head, which had assumed no responsibility for the passion I was feeling for Ed's delectable firm body.

CHAPTER 10

Exhausted from our lovemaking, I succumbed to sleeping over, something I loathed doing because I knew Tank would be up in paws the next day after missing a single precious meal, and would treat me like a scarlet letter was imprinted on my forehead. I did get up much earlier than I wanted to, just to race home and feed the spoiled fatness the leftover fish, and then drove all the way back to Fort Bragg to see Richard Powers.

Considered an authority in the field, Powers had headed up the drug program for many years, testifying as an expert witness in numerous drug trials throughout the county. Pot growers had taken over where bootleggers had left off in the county's more rural areas, but I knew that heroin had also been brought into the port in Fort Bragg and other secluded landings since the late 1800s. Richard would know the latest dope.

At his office on the northwest end of town, the receptionist asked if I could wait a few minutes until he finished with a client. I did, busying myself reading pamphlets about new designer drugs, prevention programs, treatments for addiction, and a list of all the anonymous 12-step meetings available along the coast.

Richard stepped into the waiting room and greeted me with a warm handshake. We knew each other casually, since I call him when I'm working on a case requiring superior knowledge of drugs and their effects on users.

We walked through a maze of hallways, past dozens of doors to other sections of the public health department, to Richard's cubicle in the massive complex. His walls were covered with drug-prevention posters and AA slogans. I sat on the couch across from his desk, which was piled high with file folders and what looked like drug-prevention kits for use in the public school systems.

Short and wiry, Richard was about my age and, like Ed, another aspiring athlete. For his height, it was always a mystery to me that he'd chosen to coach girls' basketball at the high school. The majority of his players were at least a foot taller than him. Despite his height disadvantage, his teams made it to the playoffs every year.

"What brings you here today, Syracuse?" Richard asked.

"I'm trying to find out all I can about heroin on the coast these days: what it's like, where it comes from, who uses it, that kind of thing," I said.

"Can I ask you why?"

"Let's just say an acquaintance of mine just OD'd on it."

"Would it be someone named Spencer?" he asked, a knowing look on his serious face.

"How'd you know?"

"Corry has to report all the overdoses to Public Health. He called me yesterday, so I assume it must be your friend."

"What do you think?" I asked. So far, Richard seemed to be the one conducting the interview. I was hoping to turn the conversation around.

"Some of this is confidential, Syracuse, but I trust your professional discretion."

Not if you knew about a certain sheriff's deputy and the kind of conduct I explicitly engaged in last night, I thought, but let him continue.

81

"Heroin has killed four people in this county in the past two weeks, all victims of Mexican black tar, a gooey, crudely processed, and deceptive type of heroin."

"What the hell is it? Sounds like something for patching roofs when the rains finally hit," I said good-humoredly.

"It makes its way into California through a human pipeline. The main trouble with black tar—and that's exactly what it looks like; not white, like the old "China White" variety—is that people don't know what they're getting. A dose can be so much stronger than China White that even longtime users can overdose. A user can buy 4 percent pure heroin today and use it without incident, but tomorrow's purchase might be 70 percent pure and kill him in an instant," he said, snapping his fingers to accent the point.

"Shit. Why the hell do they take the chance? Don't sound like very good odds to me," I said hoarsely.

"Answer that for you and I'd be solving one of life's biggest secrets. Another unknown about black tar, just as with other drugs, is what it might have been cut with, you know, what substances were mixed into the drug to increase the quantity and raise the profit margin. White-powder drugs like cocaine are cut with lactose—milk sugar. The tar, being black, is stretched with anything from vinegar to shoe polish, so it isn't always the drug itself that kills, but rather the substances used in the cutting process," he said.

"What were the people like that OD'd recently?"

"I don't know anything about the Spencer kid yet, but the other three were all habitual heroin users. They were all unemployed and transient. I don't think any of them knew what they were shooting unless they were intentionally out to kill themselves," Richard said solemnly.

"So, in other words, this black tar is potentially lethal and its potency so irregular that it's easy for someone to shoot up a dose more powerful than he can handle?" I echoed.

"Yes. Sometimes the rush is a lot more than they expect. Their respiratory and cardiovascular systems shut down and that's it," he said.

"Is it only black tar that's killing people?" I asked.

"Only because it's the only kind of heroin available up here right now."

"How do you buy the stuff? Don't get me wrong; I'm not looking to score, just curious. What's it look like, other than tar?"

"You can buy match-head-sized globs, about 100 milligrams, wrapped in aluminum foil. They sell for twenty to twenty-five dollars, which isn't much for enough high-grade heroin to keep a junkie high all day. The flow of black tar is on the rise, and competition is pushing the potency up and prices down, because the product makes its Mexican producers and American dealers rich. Broken down into 100 milligram match-heads, a kilogram—a little over two pounds—of crudely processed high-purity tar brings about a quarter-million dollars."

"Whoa! That's a lot of dough for a small package," I exclaimed.

He nodded in agreement and added, "You bet, and dope dealers willing to do a little more work can buy a kilo of 60 percent pure tar for about 150 thousand, cut it until it's only 4 percent pure, and sell it for a million and a half."

"Can you buy it by the gram, like cocaine?"

"Sure. Costs about sixty to seventy-five dollars a quarter gram, or 170 to 250 for a full gram. I doubt the potency ever exceeds 10 percent; typically it's about 3 to 4. That's why it's so easy to overdose if a typical user who's used to the lower potency gets some that hasn't been cut so much."

"So the poppies are grown in Mexico, processed into black tar, and brought into California through Mexican drug families and their associates in the good old USA," I said bitterly.

"Yes. As newcomers take up dealing here and competition increases, the chances that sloppy handling and cutting will put more dirty and high-potency tar on the market increase," he added.

"Are you seeing a rise in heroin use?" I asked. This was all fascinating to me, and I wanted to know more about it.

Enthused about sharing his knowledge, Richard continued: "Methamphetamine, cocaine, and marijuana are still more popular, but heroin use is increasing. Some experts think it will continue to rise, especially when the economy falls. Cocaine and meth are uppers, and have been used while the economy's been on an upswing. Historically, in this country we go through periods of uppers and downers, and some experts in the field say we're gearing up for another downer cycle, which will entail an increase in both the supply and potency of heroin, while at the same time reducing the price."

"I could never get past the idea of using a needle. Do you think that stops some people from experimenting with heroin?"

"Not any more. You can smoke it," he replied.

"Christ. More better living through chemistry."

After thanking Richard for the crash course in black tar heroin, I headed south for Anne's house. I decided not to call first, sure she'd be there, making preparations for Billy's funeral, and I couldn't let even the risk of encountering Frank Spencer stop me from talking to her. Although my mind was churning with thoughts of trucks, heroin, Billy's death, and how they might all connect, I allowed some prurient reflections during the drive back up the coast as I passed the sheriff's office, playing back the tape of last night's roll in the hay, careful to keep my car from drifting onto the shoulder of the road.

It took every ounce of ancient Catholic restraint I had left to drive by without pulling in for a quickie, as if that were even a possibility at a station crawling with deputies. I reminded myself that I must be ovulating, and God's sense of humor was challenging my better judgment, in His attempt to continue to populate the planet.

CHAPTER 11

Armed with the new information from Richard Powers about Mexican black tar heroin, I was beginning to question my previous assumption that Billy had been murdered. He was a druggie, but just because he smoked pot, it wasn't reasonable to conclude that he also used heroin. If he did, though, it was possible he'd accidentally done a stronger dose than he was accustomed to. Corry said he didn't have tracks on his arms, but Billy might have been smoking it.

A blue Mercedes sedan was parked in the circular driveway at the Spencer conclave, its trunk lid thrust open, as was the front door of the Phelps residence. I parked behind the sedan, stepped out of my Volvo, and headed for the entry just as a tall, slender man with his back to me entered the home, carrying two large suitcases. He put them down just inside the door, turned around and walked toward me. He was wearing pleated gray flannel slacks and a very expensive cashmere sweater the color of a pink carnation, which softened his tanned face and rugged features. He was elegant, refined, and middle-aged, with silver sideburns and highlights of silver throughout his immaculately combed brown hair. His august bearing inspired reverence.

"Hello. May I help you?" he said, addressing me as I imagined he would a door-to-door salesman, politely, but not too inviting.

"Yes, I'd like to speak with Anne," I answered.

"May I say who is calling?"

"Syracuse." *This must be Anne's husband, the early alarm system,* I thought, as he turned and went back into the house. I heard him call up the stairs to Anne and announce my name.

"She'll be right down. Would you like to come in and have a seat while you are waiting?" He offered in a friendly yet guarded manner.

"Sure. Uh, I assume you must be Mr. Phelps, Anne's husband?"

" Yes, I am. I'm sorry; I should have introduced myself. We just got back and I'm exhausted. Roger. Roger Phelps. Very nice to meet you," he said, smiling ever so slightly and extending a hand to shake mine. I didn't have a clue as to whether he had any idea who I was, or more importantly, what I did for a living and the fact his wife was more or less my client. I stepped into the foyer with a subtle but hasty motion, in case Phelps decided to dismiss me like Spencer had, figuring it would be harder to throw me out if I was already a little farther inside.

Sufficiently rooted in the entry hall, I looked up when I heard Anne's footsteps descending the wooden staircase. Here eyes were swollen as if she had been crying, but she smiled when she caught sight of me, a look of relief spreading over her face. On impulse and trained instinct, I opened my arms to her and she moved forward into my embrace. I held her for a few moments while she sobbed quietly. Phelps remained standing a few feet away, out of my line of sight, so I couldn't read his reaction to Anne's response to my arrival. I had no idea whether Spencer had confided in him about my detecting in their lives.

Disengaging from our embrace, Anne and I moved into the adjacent living room area. She was attired in another one of her preppy outfits, this time cable-stitched knee-high socks the same color as her sweater, and penny loafers. Her skirt was a tartan plaid.

"Why don't I put on some water for tea while you two catch up?" Phelps offered.

"Thank you, Roger. That would be very nice," Anne said, wiping her eyes with a handkerchief she'd been wringing in her hands.

The room was elegantly appointed with only the finest art deco furniture and fixtures; black leather and chrome dominated. Original pieces, the leather was finely broken in and more comfortable than any chair I'd ever sat in, including all the ones I'd auditioned last spring at San Francisco's leading furniture stores when I thought I was going to redecorate my office—until I balked at the prices.

Lamps and sculptures throughout the room looked like they'd been swept off the pages of *Architectural Digest* into the Phelps' living room. Black antelopes and panthers in stately poses held small, high-intensity light bulbs behind foggy globes. The all-natural rock fireplace cast gleaming light onto the glass-covered black lacquer coffee table situated between the couch where Anne sat and my sumptuous chair opposite.

On closer inspection, I noted the art prints on the walls were not reproductions, but originals by the masters of cheesecake, Rolf Armstrong, Zoe Moser, and Vargas, all set in triple mat boards, corners cut in intricate patterns, echoing and accentuating specific angles in the pictures.

"I was very sorry to hear about Billy," I said gently, as an opening remark.

"Yes. Thank you. It's awful, and I don't understand how it could have happened."

Softly, I asked, "Do you know if he ever used heroin?"

"No. I know he had a problem with marijuana, but as far as I know he never used heroin," she said, wiping her eyes again.

"Anne, why haven't you called me? I've been trying to reach you for days," I asked patiently, hoping she had an explanation.

"Roger and I have been out of the country since the day after I spoke with you. Roger is an international importer. He's away on business much of the time, and Father thought it would be good for me to get away for a few days with him. We were in Canada. I wanted to speak with you, but I knew we would be back soon. I intended to call you today, but here you are."

"Do you know about the chat I had with your father, that he wants me off this case?"

"He said he was going to talk with you. He thought it would be better for me if the entire situation were dropped, since it didn't appear to be of any significance." She seemed calm, almost too relaxed for someone who was already troubled and now additionally facing her brother's demise.

"How do you feel about it now?" I asked, hoping she would overrule her father's declaration.

"Considering what's happened with Billy, I would like to continue to retain you, only I would also like you to look into the circumstances surrounding his death," she said, becoming teary-eyed again.

Phelps stepped into the room, carrying a silver platter with matching tea service and three cups with saucers. The silver glowed with the soft patina of age. He put the tray on the coffee table, served the three of us, and sat on the couch beside Anne.

"Anne, may I assume Mr. Phelps knows I am in your employ? You understand anything we discuss is strictly confidential so it's up to you whether you want your husband present while we talk." I glanced over at Phelps. "No offense, Mr. Phelps; I just want to be certain that you both understand the issue of confidentiality."

"Roger knew I had spoken with a detective. Until now, he didn't know it was you. I share everything with my husband, and it is perfectly all right with me to discuss our business with Roger," she answered firmly.

"Good. Then we can proceed," I said, taking a sip of delicious raspberry tea laced with thick cream before I continued. "This is wonderful tea, Mr. Phelps, perhaps you have missed your calling.

"Please call me Roger. Thank you. The tea is something special I picked up in France last month. It's so good I may have to consider it as a new item to import," he said brightly.

"What do you import, if you don't mind my asking?"

"Jewelry is my main line," he answered quickly.

"Where else do you trade besides Canada and France?"

"Virtually everywhere, or so it seems: India, China, Italy, Thailand, Africa, and Mexico to name a few places. I've set up factories using designs artists here conceptualize. I deliver the prototypes and have reproductions made with native materials and an inexpensive labor force," he explained further.

"Sounds fascinating, and it looks profitable, too," I said politely with a wave around the showcase room.

"My only complaint is I am required to be away from home much more than I care to be. I hope to be able to take Anne with me more often. The separations are difficult. That's why we moved up here with Anne's parents, so she wouldn't be alone so much of the time," he added, unexpected tenderness in his voice.

I was trying to figure out how to explain to Anne how I had met her brother, and decided to just tell it straight, my visit, our aborted meeting at the beach, and my inquisitiveness about why Billy had wanted to speak with me. After I'd brought both of them up to date, Phelps spoke first.

"Well, I certainly have no idea why he wanted to talk with you. Do you, Anne?" I noticed he reached out for her hand and held it while he talked.

"No. I don't know, either," she said softly.

"What more can you tell me about Billy? He seemed so different from the rest of your family. Quite frankly, I would never have guessed he was related to you," I said, hoping to get some clarity.

"Again, Syracuse, I must rely on your professional ethics to refrain from speaking about our family business outside of this room," Phelps said sternly. "Billy came from a little indiscretion on Anne's mother's part. She had a brief affair with another man during her marriage to Frank, and Billy was the result. At the time, Elizabeth and Frank thought it would be best to bring up Billy as though Frank were his father. This was over twenty-five years ago, when abortions were not routinely used for birth control. Frank had always wanted a son, so they decided to keep the baby rather than give it up for adoption and face the embarrassment of Frank's business associates knowing his wife had made a grievous error."

"That explains a great deal," I said.

"Yes." Anne added. "Billy was a pretty good kid until he reached his teens, and then he got involved with drugs and began to cause Mother and Father nothing but grief. He was arrested several times, but Father always managed to keep it quiet, and hired excellent attorneys to keep Billy out of jail."

"Speaking of your mother, Anne, I understand she is in the hospital. Can you tell me more about that?" This was where I was afraid to tread, thinking Anne would clam up, since mental disorders are always hard for families to discuss, especially families with the kind of class this clan possessed.

Anne looked at Roger, then spoke unenthusiastically: "Mother has been having a difficult time for years. I don't know exactly what is wrong with her, what labels the doctors are using today, but she had a breakdown about a month ago and tried to commit suicide by ingesting too many sleeping pills. Her doctor decided it would be safer if she were hospitalized where she could have sufficient therapy and round-the-clock care."

"Can she have visitors?"

"Not really. Father has seen her some, but she is heavily

sedated and doesn't say much. Father just sits quietly in the room with her."

"Have you been to see her?"

"No."

"Will she be coming to Billy's funeral?"

"I understand the doctor is going to accompany her. He's afraid to let her out of his sight, especially now with Billy gone, so he's going to drive her up for the service, but take her right back to the hospital when it's over," she explained.

I studied Anne while Phelps refilled our teacups. Pained but calm, she was assuredly holding up better than I would have under the bizarre circumstances unfolding in her life.

"When is the funeral?" I asked.

"The day after tomorrow. There is just going to be a short service at the cemetery in Mendocino at one o'clock," Anne answered dryly.

"Do you mind if I come?" I asked gently.

"Father will throw a fit, but if you think it's important, I don't know why not. I'll try to talk with him," she said.

"It's very important to me, Anne. You see, part of my theory is that Billy may have been murdered. Whoever did it might be someone he recently got involved with up here, and might be stupid or guilty enough to attend the service. I just want to snoop around to see if anyone interesting shows up."

"Oh, my God," Anne said, burying her head in her hands.

"I'll talk to Frank, too," Phelps added. "Maybe he'll understand that it's necessary, especially if what you say is true."

I paused for a few minutes, allowing Anne time to consider my theory and compose herself.

"Did you know any of Billy's friends or acquaintances in Mendocino?"

"No. He never brought anyone to the house," Anne said, dabbing at her eyes, still trying to digest the idea that Billy could have been snuffed.

91

"Did he have anywhere in particular that he hung out, maybe a bar?"

"I think he used to go to the harbor in Fort Bragg some," she said.

"Do you have a recent picture of Billy I could borrow for a while?"

"Sure. I'll have to go upstairs for it," Anne said, and got up from the couch and walked toward the staircase. Her stride was light and elegant; I wondered how wealthy people acquired that kind of walk. Maybe she studied to be a model once, and walked around with books on her head. Whether in motion or perfectly still, her Grace Kelly looks were absolutely breathtaking.

When Anne had ascended the stairs and was clearly out of earshot, Phelps spoke up. "This has been very hard on Anne. The trip to Canada was good for her, but now the news about Billy has really devastated her. She's taking a mild tranquilizer for her nerves now, and that's why she is acting pretty calm while we talk about all of this," he said. *That explains her relaxed demeanor,* I thought.

"I'm certain she is very comforted having you here, too, Roger. You don't plan on leaving again right away do you?" I asked, partly because I was concerned about Anne's welfare, but also because I wanted to keep track of his travels.

"Unless something comes up I should be able to stay in Mendocino for at least two weeks."

"Good."

Anne returned to the room just then, with an eight-by-ten color photo of Billy in a black-and-gold frame. It was a good likeness. I wondered if it was the only day in his short life he'd managed to shave and comb his hair.

"You may keep this as long as you need to. I hope it will help."

"Thank you. I should be going now. Please call me if you can think of anything more. I'm still investigating the armored truck, but don't have anything concrete yet. I'll let you know as soon as I do."

With that, Phelps showed me to the door. I was relieved Spencer hadn't shown up in the middle of our visit. I wasn't in the mood for an encounter with him, which was bound to happen soon enough.

I drove back to the office, typed up my notes, and headed back out to Noyo Harbor to spend the rest of the afternoon showing Billy's picture to various locals and known druggies I had some acquaintance with down there. Then I hit the streets of Fort Bragg and did the same with other contacts. I didn't come up with much, but of course I had to trust and rely on information from stoners who were a paranoid and secretive bunch of losers.

I headed home to spend the evening with my furry roommate, first stopping at the fish market to pick him up a dinnertime treat. I didn't want any more guilt trips from Tank concerning my sexual needs.

CHAPTER 12

It didn't surprise me to wake to the sound of rain on the morning of Billy's funeral. It was, after all, the rainy season on the northern California coast, and since so much of the Anne Spencer Phelps case had seemed like a movie to me, why not have the funeral set be the stock rainy scene, with big black umbrellas topping everyone's black outfits in a dark and gloomy graveyard?

I left my cabin dressed accordingly: black wool slacks and black wool sweater over an old long-sleeved blouse of white oxford cloth. The pants were lined, but if I tried to wear the sweater without something underneath, I knew I would spend most of the day scratching, since I'm allergic to wool. I also grabbed a large tan umbrella and a tan trench coat. Black would have been more appropriate, but it isn't part of my limited wardrobe.

Many years ago I acquired a miniature camera I can conceal in the palm of my hand. After considerable practice, I can now discreetly shoot clear photos with it. I took it along to photograph some of the grieving guests. I loaded it with fast film in order to snap the sharpest pictures possible in the dim light of the weather conditions.

I had asked Ed to join me, thinking that between the two of us we might recognize someone relevant to the case. At the same time, I thought that if Ed showed up in his uniform it might offer me some protection in case Frank Spencer decided to throw one of his little tantrums. Ed said he'd be more than happy to accompany me, if we could meet for lunch first.

I stopped by my office and called Sally, who said we'd won half the battle. The board didn't feel it would be fair to ask the developer of the now completed tall building to shorten it due to the exorbitant cost of such a request, but they did slap a substantial fine on him. The other guy, however, was going to have to remove his plumbing pipes, and the building inspector would keep a sharp eye on him during the rest of the project. Sally was pleased. I told her I was too, rang off, and left to meet Ed.

I entered the Mendocino Café at eleven-thirty, several moments before Ed arrived. Despite the downpour, the view from the window table to the ocean beyond was still clear enough that I could make out the enormous whitecaps on the choppy sea. The rain made everything look as though viewed through a gray-tinted lens smeared with Vaseline—mystical and beautiful.

Ed strolled in wearing his khaki uniform and a dark brown, heavy wool jacket with the sheriff's insignia sewn onto the upper sleeve. He pulled up a chair next to me and we stared out at the ocean for several moments before we spoke. I felt sorry for the tourists who only come up to the village on vacation and don't have the same ocean view at home to contemplate daily, as locals do. It has a soothing effect, calming overworked, stressed-out minds.

Ed reached under the table and put his hand on mine. He stroked my fingers for a few minutes and then let his hand slide onto my thigh where he continued his work of art. It was a damn shame we had a funeral to attend and he had to be back to work right after, because there's nothing better to do on a rainy day than curl up in front of a cozy fire and make wild, passionate love.

"You thinking the same thing I am?" Ed said, grinning mischievously.

"To tell you the truth, Ed, I'm having simultaneous thoughts completely unrelated to each other. When I first looked out at our beautiful, pristine ocean, I thought, if the big oil companies ever get their way and start trying to put oil rigs out there, it's going to be over my dead body. At the same time, I thought of how wonderful it would be to have your yummy self lying on top of my live body."

"What a drag; I've got a meeting with the sheriff himself at two this afternoon, so I won't be able to rip your clothes off until late this evening. Can you wait, or do you want to blow off the funeral?"

"I can't blow it off, you know that."

"Yeah, but tell it to my lecherous body."

"I don't imagine there'll be a big crowd or a long ceremony. How about meeting at your place for dinner around seven? I'll stop by the store and pick up something to make us a nice meal if you'll offer up your bod for dessert afterward."

"Pick up some hot fudge and you've got a deal," he grinned.

Our waitress, a young woman I've known since she was in grammar school, one of my daughter's classmates, came over to take our order. We both chose chicken burritos, with an appetizer of cheese quesadillas served with guacamole, salsa, and sour cream. Ed ordered coffee, but I opted for hot chocolate, convinced it would satisfy my present urge for something decadent.

"What's goin' on at the station, Ed? Is anyone looking into the Spencer kid's death as a possible homicide, or is that still under my jurisdiction?"

"Nothing so far. Corry talked to Powers, and they both think he accidentally OD'd, so that's the assumption we're operating on."

We spent the rest of our lunch avoiding business talk, just trying to relax and enjoy our limited time together. I explained to Ed that I'd have to go home first and give Tank an adequate dinner and enough extra food to hold him over until morning, in case I got carried away and wanted to sleep over at his place, but that I shouldn't have any trouble meeting him there by seven. He said he hoped I'd get carried away, and we headed out for the cemetery.

I left my car at the café. We drove up the hill to the graveyard in Ed's green-and-white sheriff's cruiser. The rain continued its rhythmic beat on the windshield, too strongly for Ed to use the intermittent switch on the wipers. It was a short drive. We parked below the cemetery on the shoulder of the narrow street and began our ascent on foot.

The Mendocino Cemetery is perched on a hilltop overlooking the village from the northeast. Catholics occupy one end of the graveyard, and other denominations the remainder. I suspect that if I ever get serious about buying a plot, I'll choose one right along the fifty-yard line so I don't have to make a solemn commitment, but keep all the bases covered just in case. For the same reason, I'll also insist on having a Catholic priest at my deathbed to perform the last rites, in other words, my ticket to heaven.

The anticipated black umbrellas looked like a flock of giant crows hovering over an open grave, covered with an enormous black tarp, at the Protestant end of the cemetery. As we walked closer to the gathering, I noticed Spencer standing next to Anne and Roger, along with a woman who looked like an older version of Anne, so I assumed it was Elizabeth, flanked by a tall, distinguished man with thick brown hair and tortoise-shell glasses. He held a black felt hat in one hand and kept his other arm linked through Elizabeth's, in a manner suggesting that if he were to loosen his grip, she would plummet into the open pit. Spencer was on the other side of

Elizabeth, supporting her in the same fashion. The tall guy was either a relative I hadn't had the pleasure of meeting, or more likely, the doctor.

I noticed several Bank of Mendocino employees, Mildred included, and other businessmen and women from the village. There were a few people in Billy's age range, but none I recognized. I photographed all of them, as well as the doctor, Spencer, and Roger, since the opportunity was hard to pass up. I had to do this quickly from one position, and wasn't sure how well the pictures would turn out, because the service lasted all of ten minutes, so there was no way to meander and look casual at the same time. I nudged Ed and whispered, asking him if he could put a make on any of the younger mourners. He shook his head slowly in negative response.

Immediately after the ceremony ended, Spencer passed his arm duties over to Roger and stepped toward me. I recoiled instinctively, but stood my ground, grateful to have Ed at my side. Spencer's eyes were blazing; he seemed surprised and angry at the same time. His eyes darted around before he spoke.

"What the hell are you doing here?" he demanded, in his usual authoritative voice.

"Paying my last respects, sir," I answered, sarcastic on the final word.

"I thought I asked you to stay out of our business," he said, glaring, undertones of rage in his voice. I moved a little closer to Ed. I wanted Spencer to know we were here together, even though I felt the macho part of me could handle Spencer if he tried to make a physical move on me. I almost wished he would, so I could have the satisfaction of landing a few harsh blows on his pretty face.

"Anne is over twenty-one, sir; legally, she can do as she pleases. Also, I happen to be a friend of Billy's, and have every right to be here." That was stretching the truth, but I felt it was within reason.

Just then I noticed the tall, distinguished-looking man with the black hat making his way through the small crowd toward us. Anne was now supporting the other half of her mother. They were all beginning to look like a tag team competing in some bizarre sport.

"Anything wrong, Frank?" the tall man asked.

"Yes, this is the detective I talked to you about. She seems to be meddling again," he snapped.

Mr. Tall moved closer and reached out his hand to me. We shook for God only knows what reason, and for one irrational Catholic moment I felt religious significance performing this common act on the sacred burial ground.

"I am Doctor William Peterson, the Spencers' physician," he said, his bespectacled face pleasant.

"Syracuse here," I answered briefly.

"It seems we have a situation here that is extremely uncomfortable for Mr. Spencer, and frankly I don't know what to do about it, short of reiterating what he has already confided to me. Mr. Spencer thinks you are needlessly and pointlessly provoking him and his family for no apparent reason. Is that true?" he asked politely yet firmly.

His concern seemed genuine, and for a split but sincere second I was able to empathize with Spencer's plight. I was probably a pain in his ass, and this was the day of his son's funeral, but I had my investigation to take into account and felt my attendance at the service was mandatory.

"I'm sorry, Dr. Peterson, that my presence here is of such concern to Mr. Spencer. I'm only trying to do my job. Anne retained me awhile back, and I did ask her if it would be O.K. to attend the funeral, since I wanted to observe the people who came. That's all," I said, a timid look on my face.

"Why would you care who was here?"

"I thought perhaps a suspect might show up, now that it appears Billy may have been murdered."

"Murdered! Who said anything about a murder?" Peterson exclaimed.

"I did," I answered.

"Oh, no, that couldn't be. Billy was a sick and troubled young man. He was using drugs for years, in and out of jail a number of times, always being rescued by his father. The coroner determined, and I concur, that Billy overdosed on heroin, a type easy to accidentally overdose on, I understand," Peterson explained.

"We're all entitled to our opinions, doctor. This is America, y'know, as in free country," I said, noting the restraint I was employing, not wanting to fall into my smart-ass attitude in front of Spencer again, for fear that Peterson would have to side with him more vigorously if I ruffled additional feathers in this pair of potentially foul turkeys. Up to this point Peterson was being diplomatic, so I didn't see much reason to treat him with any of the contemptuous hostility I felt for Spencer.

Spencer started to say something, but Peterson held him at bay.

"Maybe for now you could just be more considerate of what the family is going through, and leave this matter to the proper authorities," Peterson said. He leaned over closer to me and in a softer voice added, "They're going through hell right now, and it's my job to treat them. Please, just be more discreet, if you could." He reached into his overcoat pocket, extracted a business card, and handed it to me. "If you wish to talk further, please call me."

With that, he and Spencer turned and headed back toward Elizabeth, to take up their positions on either side of her and escort her back to the black limo parked at the edge of the cemetery. She looked like an injured athlete being assisted off the playing field.

Anne and Roger followed behind them. Anne gave me a quick wave over her shoulder, and a small but sufficient smile as she descended the hill. Roger nodded and tipped his hat.

Ed and I followed the clan down to Ed's cruiser, careful to avoid making physical contact, even though both of us wanted to. In a small town it's best to keep personal involvement of our caliber private in public places. I was thankful Ed hadn't spoken out during my confrontation with Spencer. He knew me well enough to know I wanted to handle it myself. Ed dropped me off at my Volvo and hurried off to his meeting with the sheriff.

I stopped by the office to pick up my messages, hit the post office, picked up dinner fixings at the market, did three loads of wash at the village laundry, and drove home to feed Tank before racing back into town and Ed's house. I got to his place a good hour before he arrived, in plenty of time to start dinner and develop my film in his darkroom off the kitchen. The roll came out better than I'd expected, good, clear negatives of the entourage, from which I made contact prints and would make enlargements later.

Dinner was also a hit, pasta with pesto, a fresh green salad, and hot fudge topping applied in all the right places for dessert.

CHAPTER 13

Lucia was standing on the wood plank sidewalk in front of her store when I pulled up to park in my favorite parking place the next morning. Holding what looked like a large roll of butcher paper under her left arm, she peered up at the space between the floors of our two businesses on the building's south façade.

I stepped out of the Volvo and sauntered over. "Don't tell me, sweetie pie, you're getting ready for your annual pre-Christmas sale and you could use a hand hanging that banner across the front of the store," I said, looking smug. I recognized the banner because I had designed and lettered it for her last winter.

"You private eyes think you know everything, don't you?" she said, her face reflecting that quality of serious amusement it so often held. She stared motionless at the wall for a moment and then looked back at me. "Okay, Ms. Philip Marlowe, you're right, I could use a hand."

"Where's the ladder? You know I don't like to fly in public when I perform these supernatural acts," I said arrogantly.

"It's in the steaming room."

"Be right back." I entered the store, inhaled the scent of new leather from the ample selection of jackets and skirts, and headed for the back room. Looking around at the offerings,

I realized that in ten years Lucia had come a long way, from running a thrift store full of used garments to operating one of the most appealing and successful women's clothing stores in the area.

Dragging the ladder out onto the sidewalk, I carefully positioned it against the wall, far from any windows, before raising the second level of the extension. Patience pays off when you work near glass. I looked over at Lucia and smiled. "This reminds me of the day I put those bars on the double-hung windows at the back of the store, when you doubled in size and inventory and thought it was time to take precautions against burglars. Do you remember we both agreed there was no need to have bars on the top sections because they were so high off the ground a thief would have to bring along a ladder, and then a year later, one did just that?"

"You don't have to remind me," Lucia grumbled. She looked troubled though, even before I related the story, like she was holding something back from me, so I tried to lighten the mood.

"Sometimes I think you're secretly trying to drive me crazy with these tedious little chores you come up with," I said good-naturedly.

"No one can "drive" you crazy Syracuse, everyone knows in your case it would only be a short putt," she fired back.

"I give up, Lucia; despite my omnipotent physical powers you still trounce me verbally every time."

Secretly, I was happy to do some physical work this morning, because I'd drunk some of Ed's killer coffee and was feeling like I'd been injected with rocket fuel. I thought the coffee might help me sort out my latest ideas about the Spencer family, but at this point I was too speeded up to concentrate on any one thought for more than a few seconds, much less put them all together coherently.

Lucia held the ladder as I edged it along the front of the

building and made a slow upward climb. In eighteen-inch red letters, her banner, about forty feet long, read twenty percent off everything. I checked her reaction to my placement. Yes, it was straight and centered. When I came down after securing the final pushpin, I looked into Lucia's brown eyes, focused on mine, and I could sense her mind was elsewhere than on the banner.

"What's up, toots? Why the look? You're not still pouting over our screw-up when we didn't add those extra bars, are you?" I asked soothingly.

"I'm worried about you," she said quietly. Her silver hair gleamed in the morning sunlight, the dour look on her face contrasting with it.

"Whaddya mean?"

"I didn't want to tell you this until we got the banner up, because I knew you'd run off without helping me," she said sheepishly, "but someone broke into your office last night."

"Why the hell didn't anybody call me?" I said, annoyed.

"I just discovered it when I got here and went upstairs to change a fuse in the electrical box. I've called the sheriff; he should be here any minute," she explained.

"Christ!" I ran up the stairs. It was just like Lucia to get her damn banner up before telling me my office had been violated, but I wasn't angry with her because she was right, the banner would never have been hung today if she had, and knowledge of the break-in could wait fifteen minutes.

My wood front door looked like fodder for a toothpick factory. Whoever busted in was short on finesse or experience. It looked like it had been savagely attacked with an ax. Inside, the contents of all my desk drawers and file cabinets were spilled onto the floor, papers strewn every which way, tables overturned, lamps smashed, pictures broken, everything rummaged except for the wall safe, which they couldn't penetrate. Good thing, since that's where I keep my notes on active cases, and more importantly, my gun.

Lucia came up the stairs, followed by a young sheriff's deputy, a quiet officer, polite and unobtrusive. I told him I'd know more about what if anything had been taken once I'd had a chance to straighten things up. After telling me not to be concerned about fingerprints, since Lucia's and mine were all over the room anyway, and he could dust for prints later, he left with my promise to call this afternoon.

Lucia looked at me and said, "Syracuse, this really frightens me. Somebody might be trying to kill you."

"Naw. They were looking for something, not for me, unless they thought I sleep in my file cabinet."

"They'll go to your cabin next," Lucia said.

"No way. It's my hideout, very safe; no one knows where I live or how to find my place, except for a chosen few."

"Unless, of course, they follow you home," she retorted.

"Well, I didn't go home last night."

Her eyebrows shot up. "Oh, really? Where were you when the lights went out?"

"I'll never say." I could tell she was dying to know whom I'd spent the night with, but I wasn't ready to talk.

"I think you should call your neighbor and see if anyone broke into your cabin."

"Good idea, but I doubt it very much. I have a watch cat, y'know."

"Sure. From what I've heard, all he watches is his dish."

I called the woman who lives across the road from my cabin, told her where the key was hidden, and held the line while she went over there. She returned quickly and said everything looked intact except for a big, gray cat that was crying and complaining as though he hadn't eaten in a month, even though his dish was full. I explained to her it was his usual M.O. She said she'd fallen for it and given him a little half-and-half from the fridge to assuage his suffering. I thanked her and turned back to Lucia.

"Everything's cool," I said.

"Yeah, about as cool as a smoldering fire."

"I've got to start cleaning up this mess."

"I can have one of my employees watch the store for a while if you want me to help you straighten up. I don't mind."

"Thanks, Lucia, and please don't worry about me. This kind of thing happens all the time in my line of work. It's really no big deal," I said, in my most convincing tone.

We got the place back together by one-thirty. As far as I could tell, nothing was missing. I called the sheriff's office to relay the information to the young deputy who'd been out to my office earlier. I asked to speak to Ed, but he wasn't in.

Stored behind the building was a sheet of plywood left over from Lucia's expansion project; I dragged it up the stairs and nailed it across my doorway. Then Lucia and I strolled up Main Street, turned onto Kasten, and went to the Chocolate Moose for lunch. Following a nutritious barley soup and garden salad, we moved into the more serious segment of the meal, the tasty, rich desserts the Moose is famous for. I had a chocolate mousse puff, and Lucia chose vanilla ice cream topped with hot fudge. I didn't share the previous night's alternative applications of hot fudge with her.

We walked back to our respective businesses. I had to extract the nails to enter mine and push the plywood off to one side of the landing. Lucia said she'd have a new door put up this afternoon.

Once inside, I noticed the answering machine blinking: Ed had called, so I called him right back, assuming he wanted to talk about the break-in, but that wasn't why he'd tried to reach me. Something more important was coming down, and he asked me to get to the station as fast as I could. I did.

CHAPTER 14

"Sorry to hear about your break-in," Ed said as I entered the sheriff's office. He was perched in his usual manner, feet propped up on his desktop, a copy of the *Chronicle*'s sports section in his lap, no doubt studying the 49ers' current position in the conference standings, and which teams baseball players were signing with during the off season—and for how many millions.

"Thanks, Ed. Doesn't look like anything was taken, so I think it was just a subtle warning."

"About as subtle as a chainsaw. Do you think it was the Spencer family?"

"Maybe."

"Well, I think I've got something that might just be the break you're looking for," Ed said. He motioned for me to sit in the chair next to his desk, put his feet on the floor, and pulled his chair closer so we could speak softly in case any of the other deputies walked by.

"This looks like it must be good," I said. "Fire."

"This morning, a couple of deputies brought in two young guys charged with possession of heroin with intent to sell. They were both at Billy's funeral. They haven't been interrogated yet, won't be until the narcotics squad gets here later. I thought you might want to have first crack at them, remembering, of course, that my ass won't be worth shit if you tell anyone I let you in on this."

I couldn't help it—I jumped out of my chair and kissed him firmly on the lips.

"I won't ask how I can thank you, that'll come later. Where are they?"

"I've got them in a holding cell in the back, by Corry's office. Their names are John Merlino and Tony Natoli, both in their early twenties and Fort Bragg natives from old pioneer families."

"Enough Italian names in one sentence to cook a pot of minestrone soup," I said. Ed chuckled, put his arm through mine, and escorted me to the cell, then brought back a chair for me to use while I interviewed them, a wall of steel bars separating us. Without saying a word to the pair, he left.

They looked much the same as the boys I grew up with in the Italian section of Syracuse, New York. They could have been half brothers or cousins, their features were so similar: olive skin, jet-black wavy hair, aquiline noses, small mustaches; they even dressed alike, jeans and flannel shirts over dark turtlenecks. To me, they were *paisans,* and despite their predicament, intuition told me they'd gotten in over their heads unintentionally. My Italian heritage led me to believe I could trust them and pressed me into a protective stance—all this and I hadn't even talked to them yet.

I pulled my chair closer to the cell and spoke quietly. "My name's Syracuse. I'd like to talk to you guys for a few minutes. I know you got yourselves in a jam here, and I might be able to help you out." Silence from their side of the bars, so I went on. "I'm not a cop. I'm a private investigator. I have a lot of friends in the court system here, including the district attorney who's going to prosecute you. I also have a lot of friends who are judges."

Their silence continued, so I tried a new tack: "I can talk to my friends and put in a good word for you if you'll help me out. You're going to be found guilty, because the evidence against you is bigger than shit. You'll do time, because the judges around here aren't exactly crazy about heroin dealers. If you help me, I might be able to get you off with probation and maybe a stint in a chemical dependency recovery facility, which is a lot better place to hang out than prison, unless you guys are aspiring convicts."

Throughout my monologue they looked down at the concrete floor without responding.

"For Christ's sake, you guys, I'm Italian!" I almost screamed. "Do you think I'm going to fuck you over, or something? For what?"

They looked at one another. After a long silence, one of them finally spoke. "How do we know we can trust you?"

"I swear on the grave of my mother," I said, appealing to our common heritage. A genuine Italian would never use that expression in jest. I meant it, too, and it worked. The boys understood its significance and finally opened up.

"O.K., whaddya wanna know?"

First, who are you, which is which, who's who?"

"I'm Tony, he's Johnny," one said, nodding toward the other.

"Does either of you know the late Billy Spencer? I assume you must, because I saw you at his funeral."

"I thought you looked familiar," Tony said. "Yeah, he was an acquaintance of ours."

"Did you kill him?"

"For Christ's sake, lady, what the hell you think we are?"

"I don't know. That's what I'm trying to figure out."

They continued to look at one another for guidance. Tony seemed to be the spokesman, probably the leader, who made most of the decisions for the duo.

I continued my line of questioning. "Where did you get the heroin you were selling? Did you get it from Billy, or did you sell any of it to him?"

"No to both, lady. Billy didn't do smack, only weed."

"Where'd you get it, then? Don't freak; I won't tell anyone, I promise."

Tony looked at Johnny, who nodded. "You're not gonna believe it, lady. I swear, you're not gonna believe it."

"Try me."

"You swear you won't talk, not tell anybody about this?"

"I've said so in as many ways as I can, Tony. Trust me: you do me a favor; I do you a favor, the old Italian custom, y'know. You can trust me. I ain't gonna fuck you." Christ, I was slipping into street jargon.

"I think she's okay Tony," Johnny said, his first words to utter.

"O.K., here goes. Johnny and me been watchin' the armored trucks around town, thinkin' if we could bust into one it would set us up for life. It was kinda like a dream we had, y'know? We're not really thugs, we've never done any really big jobs like that. Anyways, we knew one armored truck went up Little Lake Road every Saturday, so we go out there and wait. When it was comin', Johnny lays down in the road like he was hit by a car or somethin'. The truck driver pulls into a turnout and gets out to see what's wrong. Then I pull up my pickup and block his truck. I jump out with my gun—Johnny had one too—and we hold the guards at gunpoint while they open up the back of the truck. There was only a few moneybags inside, but we figured it'd be enough for us. We took the guards' guns and blew outta there fast as we could."

I looked at the two of them, astounded by the story.

"Great. So now you're millionaires, but you get caught pulling some dumb stunt when you got all the money in the world. Not too bright, boys."

"No, lady, you don't get it. We get back to our place, open the bags, and there ain't no money in 'em."

"Uh-huh," I said attentively. "I suppose they were full of birdseed."

"No, lady, they was full of bundles of heroin," he muttered in a low voice.

"Jesus fucking Christ! Excuse me, guys; excuse me, Christ. So you decided to cut your losses by selling it, 'cause you didn't make any money pulling off the heist?"

"That's right."

"What's your connection with Billy?"

"We hung out some with him down at the harbor, smoked a little pot. He's the one we told we wanted to hit a truck, and he seen the one that went up Little Lake Road every Saturday and told us about it."

"Did he expect a cut?" I asked?

"We was gonna give him one when we scored."

"Did you sell any of the heroin besides what you sold to the narc?"

"Naw, not a dime," Tony answered.

"Boys, I got two things to say to you: first, don't tell anyone we had this talk, and I mean no one, not even the cops. Second, I'll do everything I can to get you the best attorney in town and try to keep you out of jail. Under the circumstances, I think you've got a good chance of beating the rap."

"You do?" Tony said.

"Yeah. Now, one other thing: until I can figure out who you ripped off, I'd guess there are at least two, and no doubt their ringleader, who are probably in hot pursuit of your asses, so when you get out on bail, I suggest you find a good place to hide out and lay very low. If you don't have a place, you can stay at my cabin. Here's my card. Call me if you need to."

"Gee, lady, you're really O.K. Thanks a lot," Johnny spoke again.

"Don't forget to call me if you need help." With that, I left.

Ed was talking to several deputies by the front door, so, before they could spot me, I turned and headed for the rear exit, figuring the fewer people who knew I'd been back there, the safer I'd be until I could wrap this raw information into a nice, tidy package.

If Tony and Johnny were telling the truth, the outside pieces of my puzzle were firmly in place, and all I had to do was fill in the center of the challenging and exciting riddle. Adrenalin was surging through my veins. I'd reached the point of no possible return in the case, and felt the accompanying exhilaration, which both inspired me and produced an intoxication that put the best bourbon to shame.

As soon as I returned to the office, I called the best criminal lawyer on the coast, Jenny O'Reilly, and retained her to represent the boys. I figured I could write it off on my expense account, since they'd played such a major role in this drama.

CHAPTER 15

Santa Rosa is about two hours southeast of Mendocino, via a stretch of road perched high above the coastline on cliff tops with breathtaking ocean views. The road then winds through redwood forests, grows in width as it passes through an agricultural valley, and finally joins Highway 101 on its descent into the expanding city. Carsickness is the most common complaint while making this trek, because the curves never let up. I can usually make it without pit stops for motion sickness, but my weak bladder usually demands one stop in Cloverdale, just half an hour short of Santa Rosa, especially after I've had the mandatory cup of coffee for the road.

The case was finally beginning to show signs of coming together. I was grateful for the drive today; it would give me time to mull things over. My intent was to visit Elizabeth, to determine if she could help me at all, and to have four hours, round trip, of alone time in my Volvo sanctuary to do what I do best—sing at the top of my voice to opera on the tape deck while figuring out whodunit.

I made my final pass along the ocean and entered the first of a series of redwood forests. The hard rains and stiff winds had dumped piles of branches along the roadside; road crews had swept them to one side, to be cut into smaller sections and hauled away when they could get to it.

During the lull between storms, forest creatures can be seen in abundance, especially deer. I thought either their sense of smell was keener with the additional moisture in the air, or they were in search of a watering hole provided by Mother Nature. Each time a deer sprinted across the road in front of me, I slowed to a crawl, because deer tend to travel in pairs, and a second one would be stepping out shortly to follow its buddy. Colliding with deer is so common here that whenever somebody hits one, people ask if it was the motorist's first time—as if a shortage of virgin deer-killers resided in the county.

I got to Cloverdale at eleven o'clock, used the restroom at a combination gas station and mini-mart, and picked up a snack to keep my ulcer at bay, along with a cup of coffee laced heavily with cream. I looked at my directions once more to be sure I wouldn't miss the exit for the hospital on the north side of Santa Rosa, about twenty minutes away.

Anticipating today's game plan, I dressed in one of my best outfits—actually my only best outfit: black pants and jacket over a white rayon blouse. Gold earrings and pin completed the ensemble, all put together expertly by Lucia, who'd loaned me a pair of black shoes, since tennis shoes and loafers make up my personal collection of footwear. I'd also packed a white medical jacket, fake wire-rimmed eyeglasses with clear lenses, and an official-looking clipboard with bogus medical forms attached. A defunct beeper was clipped to my waistband, in full view as long as I left the jacket casually open.

The hospital was smaller than I'd hoped; I wanted to go unnoticed, and its size was going to make that part of my plan difficult, although easier to find Elizabeth and allow for a fast getaway if necessary.

With an air of confidence and superiority, I approached the receptionist, inwardly praying that Dr. Peterson was out to lunch, playing golf, or otherwise occupied.

"Dr. Leventhal here to see Mrs. Elizabeth Spencer," I announced in a firm, businesslike tone to the secretary, an attractive young woman with the longest fingernails I'd ever seen, and red lipstick to match. I wondered how the hell she typed with those claws. She ran her pointy finger down the list of patients until she reached "Spencer," then ran the lethal tip horizontally to the column indicating room numbers. I could read them upside down—and the notation stipulating no visitors.

"Room 313, down this hall and to your left at the end," she said, once again utilizing the crimson pointer. Thank God she wasn't giving pelvic examinations in this place.

"Thank you," I said, nodding professionally.

Not wanting to waste a moment, I walked briskly down the hall to Elizabeth's room. I stood outside for a few seconds to be certain no one was in the room with her. I was beginning to wish I had worn more of a disguise, in case Frank Spencer showed up.

Slowly and as quietly as possible I turned the door handle and stepped into the room. The woman I had seen propped up by her two flankers at the funeral was sitting very still in a chair by the window, staring out through blank, unmoving eyes. I approached her cautiously. She hadn't yet even noticed I'd entered the room, though I was well within her peripheral vision. After several attempts to engage her verbally, I realized it didn't take a genius to know she was virtually comatose. I couldn't get any response, neither verbal nor physical, not even a blink from her torpid blue eyes. She was either heavily seated, totally cuckoo, or both. No point prolonging this one-sided conversation, but as long as I was in her room, I decided to look around for something to tell me what kind of medication she was on and what her prognosis was.

I didn't find a chart, but on a bedside table next to a plastic water pitcher and cup was a small paper cup with a single orange capsule in it. I picked it up and wrote down the code number stamped on it, Lilly F40, to look up in my *Physician's Desk Reference* when I got back home. Not wanting to push my luck, I figured I'd better get the hell out of there.

I stuffed the medical jacket and glasses into my purse, thinking if I got caught now, it would be better to be me than an imposter. There wasn't a rear exit—no surprise in a mental ward—so I left the way I'd come, avoiding the receptionist when I slipped past her. I breathed a sigh of relief as I made my way down the hospital stairs to my car in the adjacent parking lot.

As I was unlocking the car door, I felt a hand suddenly come to rest on my shoulder. I turned quickly to face whoever was intruding on my personal space.

"What brings you here, Syracuse?" Dr. Peterson asked, removing his hand.

"Oh, hi, Dr. Peterson. I was hoping to see Mrs. Spencer, but I was told she can't have any visitors," I said, in the most courteous tone I've used since my days of hitting the confessionals on Saturday afternoons, hoping Peterson wouldn't ask "crimson nails" about me.

"You do get around, don't you?"

"Yeah. I was hoping Mrs. Spencer could tell me a little about Billy's friends, but it's O.K., I can check around up in Fort Bragg."

"Listen, I'm sorry about the way I talked with you at the funeral, but Mr. Spencer too is a patient of mine, and I felt like I had to come to his defense. He's really a pretty nice guy; he's just going through an awful lot right now, and I could tell he needed some support because of the way you two were going at each other."

"Well, it's a problem, because Anne hired me to investigate her brother's death, and it's kinda hard to do that without getting in Spencer's way now and again."

"Frank's really under a lot of pressure. He recently moved to Mendocino from Los Angeles, seeking a quieter lifestyle, and then his wife, as I'm sure you know, tried to commit suicide. To top things off, his son died. He's just trying to get his life back together, and seems to think you're meddling in his affairs."

"I'll do my best to keep out of his way," I said reassuringly.

"Good. He's even thinking of getting a restraining order against you, so if I were you I would tread softly. I realize Anne wants you to pursue the matter, but didn't the sheriff say Billy's death was an accident?"

"I'm not so sure," I said, unwilling to share any of my hunches.

Peterson looked at his watch, then said, "Please look at the entire picture and then make your decisions. I have to make my rounds now, but it was nice to talk to you again, this time in more pleasant surroundings and circumstances."

"Likewise. Here's my card. In case there's anything you'd like to talk to me about," I said, "call me."

"Thanks. I don't get up to Mendocino much, but when I do, maybe we could meet for coffee. And if I can be of any help to you, give me a call. You can get my number through the hospital here."

"Sure. Thanks."

Peterson turned and walked off toward the hospital. I started up the Volvo and headed back for the freeway, delighted to have a couple more hours of uninterrupted puzzle solving in the comfort of my sturdy vehicle.

During the return trip I went over all the information I had on the case, and deduced that everyone involved with the bogus armored truck that got me into this crazy investigation in the first place, and with Billy's death, was a suspect.

Someone was hauling heroin around in an armored truck, for God knows what reason, unless Tony and Johnny were lying. Since Spencer was a bank president, and an asshole, it seemed logical to conclude he was supplementing his income by running a drug business on the side, using his idea of a company car. Maybe Billy wanted a cut and threatened to expose him, so Spencer had him killed by the fake bank guards, who were out for blood anyway, because somebody had ripped them off. If Spencer was orchestrating this symphony, he was a fool to think he could wave his baton for long in a village as small as Mendocino, where everyone knows everyone else's business.

Enter Roger, exporter and importer, a man in a perfect position to bring heroin into the States under the umbrella of his jewelry business. If that was the case, though, his wife was blowing his cover, which indicated either he was innocent or didn't confide in his wife all the intricate details of his business dealings. Maybe they were in cahoots, but then why would Anne have come to me in the first place, knowing that I, the omniscient detective who could easily solve any crime, might eventually bust them? Maybe she'd hired me thinking I'd lead her and Roger to the guys who ripped them off, so they could get their heroin back.

I pulled into the same gas station I'd used on my drive south, to pee again, pick up some more coffee, and make a phone call to Anne, who answered on the second ring. I told her I had some new information and asked if she could meet me in the village around five o'clock. She suggested the Mendocino Hotel's sitting room, which suited me. For once, I was dressed properly for the sophisticated crowd that frequented the establishment.

During the rest of the drive up the coast, I decided none of the people I knew were suspects, and the real culprits were unknowns. My next thought was to give up the case to the sheriff's department, quit private detecting, go into semi-retirement, and sell a little real estate on the side. These considerations only occur to me when a case starts stretching my brain cells like muscles desperately in need of a less strenuous form of exercise. The only other time I've felt this way was when I was forced to take statistics in graduate school, a subject I couldn't even pronounce, much less comprehend.

Just as I pulled into Mendocino, the rain began to fall again. This time the heavens offered a soothing rhythm, as opposed to the hard-driving downpours that turn locals into sprinters. I stopped in to say hi to Lucia before going up to my office. Knowing she was concerned after the break-in, I thought she needed a little reassurance, especially as I'd been gone all day.

Lucia's store was void of customers, I guessed because of the recent rains we'd been having. The weather was keeping tourists from making the drive to the coast. Lucia was reclining on the store couch, eyes shut, and an open magazine across her lap. Hearing footsteps, she blinked her eyes open.

"Slow day, huh, kiddo?" I said, walking toward her.

"I've read the entire *Chronicle* and even took a catnap."

"Maybe you should put up a self-serve sign," I quipped. The rain suddenly picked up, and the lights began to flicker as the wind increased in velocity.

"If the power goes out, I'm going home to my cats and a good book. Where the hell have you been?"

"Had to run to Santa Rosa."

"That young deputy came by and dusted for prints. He asked if I knew where you were. Only served to worry me," she said.

"Anyone else come by?"

Lucia pulled herself up to a sitting position. I sat down next to her on the couch and waited for her retort.

"Are you ever going to get a secretary, or are you planning to put me on the payroll next month?" she asked, though I knew she didn't mean a word of it.

"C'mon, I know it's a slight inconvenience, but think of all I do for you."

"Yeah. You cause me heartache and grief. Every time you get to a certain stage in a case, someone either wires a bomb to your ignition or breaks into your office with an ax."

She was serious now, but there wasn't much I could do or say to lessen her concern. I loved my work. There were risks in life all the time, no matter what one's occupation.

"No one else came by that I know of; of course, I might have missed something when I fell asleep, and I can't see the staircase from the couch. Why don't you go up and see if someone pinned a note on the new front door I had installed. You'll love it: it's made of brick; guaranteed to keep out the big bad wolf, but it'll be the first thing to go if we have an earthquake up here."

"Let's have dinner tonight. I need a little relaxation. Why don't you call up Harriet and Larry and see if they'd be up for a game of pinochle. We could meet them after dinner."

Her face brightened. "Can you meet me at the store at six-thirty?"

"I've got a five o'clock appointment at the hotel, but that should leave me plenty of time. See you then," I said. I started out the door, but was stopped by her next question. Out of the blue, she asked, "Whom are you sleeping with?"

"Why do you ask?"

"Don't give me that shit," she shot back.

"Ed, if it makes any difference to you."

"That's what I thought. Didn't you learn your lesson the last time around with him?"

"When it comes to matters of the heart, Lucia, we have absolutely no sense. I'm in lust with the guy, not in love, and that makes even less sense," I added, and popped outside.

My new office door was beautiful: solid oak nearly two inches thick, with deadbolts as well as a chain lock. It took me the rest of the afternoon to type up my notes, which I then put in the wall safe with the others. The Mendocino Hotel was only a block away, so I left at exactly 4:55 to meet with Anne. Fortunately, the rain had subsided, so the walk didn't involve extensive rain gear.

The hotel sits on Main Street, on prime ocean-view property that most real estate agents would give their eyeteeth to list. A crew of industrious gardeners landscaped its massive gardens to perfection year round. The architecture is Victorian, with yellow clapboard siding, and enormous entry doors with beveled glass in intricate tulip patterns. A glass-walled patio sits adjacent to the main building protecting diners from sea winds and frequent rains. Tea dances are occasionally featured in the patio room, which boasts a small but adequate hardwood dance floor.

The ceiling of the main dining room houses several stained-glass windows, and the area separating the bar from the restaurant has additional beveled and etched window partitions. A sitting area adjacent to the dining area has a wonderful old tin fireplace, surrounded by ornate overstuffed chairs and couches. Card tables are stacked with chess and other board games for guests to play by the warm fire.

The flowery red wallpaper, and someone's attempt to match it with even more flowery red drapes in a slightly different pattern, is the hotel's worst feature. Every time I see it I have an irresistible urge to either rip down the curtains or start priming the walls for a solid color of paint.

Anne was sitting in one of the chairs near the fireplace; no one else was in the sitting room. As I approached, she turned, and then stood to greet me with an embrace. We sat near one another in plush oversized chairs.

"I'm so glad you called," Anne said. "I've wanted to speak with you ever since the funeral. I'm really sorry for Father's behavior. He wasn't very nice to you, and I hope you'll accept my apology."

"No need, Anne, he's just doing what he seems to think is right."

A waitress came over from the bar to ask if we wanted cocktails. I ordered a bottle of mineral water with a twist of lime; Anne asked for the same. Christ—the goddamn plants in my office hadn't been watered since the last time Anne and I had a drink; the poor things will probably dry up and die before my very own private eyes.

"I have some new information regarding the case," I began, with just a suggestion of pride. "I can't give you all the details yet, because it might endanger some lives, but I've found a witness who saw the armored truck on Little Lake Road the same day you did." Before continuing, I checked around the room to be certain no one had entered. I lowered my voice "And I've also discovered who the two guys were that held up the truck, so you really did see what you thought you saw, and you're not cuckoo after all."

Before Anne could respond, the waitress came over and deposited our drinks on the mahogany coffee table in front of our chairs. I gave her five bucks and told her to keep the change. I thought I was being generous, but for all I knew, this classy joint might charge that much for a glass of tap water.

"Oh, Syracuse, that's wonderful news. I'm sure I must owe you some more money than the retainer, so please send me a bill for the balance," she said brightly.

"Well, I'm not finished yet. There's still the matter of Billy." I'm not convinced his death was an accident. He knew the guys who robbed the truck, and it's likely the guards who were robbed were transporting heroin instead of money, and they're probably not too happy about the heist."

"Heroin!" she exclaimed.

"Yeah, the truck was full of heroin."

"This is too much. I don't understand," she said, looking puzzled.

"Don't feel alone, neither do I."

"Are the police looking into this now?" she asked, a troubled look in her beautiful blue eyes.

"Yes. They've arrested the guys who held up the truck, but so far they're still operating on the assumption Billy's death was accidental. They haven't tied the two events together yet, that is, if they even *should* be linked."

"Oh. I see."

"Actually Anne, everything I've told you must be kept in the strictest confidence until I can sift through the rest of this mess, so please don't mention anything we've talked about to anyone, not even Roger."

"Of course. If it's that important, I won't breathe a word," she assured me.

I told Anne I'd call her if I found out anything more, and we got up to leave. We'd finished the water, so the plants wouldn't get the leftovers this time, and I headed back to the office.

I stopped in to see Lucia, who told me that Harriet and Larry had previous plans, and had postponed our pinochle date until tomorrow night. That was fine with me, because I had some late-night detecting to do, and would have had to cancel the game anyway.

CHAPTER 16

After a lovely dinner with Lucia, and my solemn promise to play pinochle the following evening, I drove home to prepare the next part of my game plan. Tank greeted me at the door, more interested in the small white bag of leftovers than in me. I poured a few dry stars into his bowl, and topped them with several chunks of snapper sautéed in butter. He wasted no time, gulping down the fish as though it had been his first meal in weeks.

I walked over to the bookcase and pulled out the *Physician's Desk Reference,* to look up the capsule I had discovered in Elizabeth's room. The book contained over 2,000 pages of prescription drugs, including a section of color photos of the more commonly prescribed medications. The orange capsule was easy to identify, using the imprinted code number.

It was Seconal, 100 milligrams, a powerful barbiturate that depresses the central nervous system, used primarily as a sedative-hypnotic. I read on. It was further described as capable of producing all levels of central nervous system mood alteration, from excitation, which I knew Elizabeth didn't exactly exemplify, to mild sedation, hypnosis, and even deep coma.

My guess was Elizabeth was getting plenty of the stuff, along with other psychotropic drugs, considering the state I'd found her in.

Having finished his meal, Tank was now bathing himself on my trench coat, which I had thrown carelessly onto the back of a chair, knowing full well he enjoyed leaving his long hairs on anything clean—the laundry basket full of freshly washed clothes was his all-time favorite perch. My coat was too good for a bath mat, so I pulled it out from under him, sending him flying to the floor, and hung the coat in the closet.

Next, I undressed, careful to hang up my good clothes and cover them with an old plastic dry-cleaning bag, and put on a pair of black jeans, a black turtleneck, dark blue fisherman's knit cap, and a heavy blue wool coat. I spent several minutes rummaging the back of the closet in search of a pair of rubber boots, finally finding them underneath some dusty old canvas suitcases.

By now Tank was asleep on the TV, so I left the cabin as quietly as I could, knowing he would throw a feline fit if he knew I was going out for yet another evening.

It was ten o'clock by the time I reached the entrance to the Spencer-Phelps complex. I parked my car on the side of the road and stashed a small flashlight in my jacket pocket. The moon was nearly full, so I wouldn't have to worry about finding my way around among the thick rhododendrons and tall redwoods. The walk from the car to the circular parking area, a good quarter mile, took me almost fifteen minutes, because I didn't want to be heard or spotted by anyone who chanced to venture outside. It was so quiet you could hear a pine needle drop. Several cars were parked in the drive, and interior lights glowed in both homes.

I had a hunch, one of those feelings not based on any fact, but too strong to ignore. In my business, one has to act on these impulses, because they so often pay enormous dividends, which is more than I can say about my ventures in the stock market.

When I got within 100 yards of the homes, I made a wide circle around the side of Spencer's palace, over to a dirt road leading to the old red barn. The pasture was short on trees, so I had to walk a great distance out of my way to stay within the protection of vegetation tall enough to conceal me. I didn't feel like crawling on hands and knees through the mud, so I opted for the longer jaunt. This caper was different from fooling around with Sally Covington—if the wrong person spotted me here, I might lose the back of my head.

The barn door had a thick padlock, and I'd forgotten to bring a single tool to deal with this sort of deterrent. I cussed under my breath. After circling the entire structure in search of other doors and windows, I discovered a smaller entrance, more like a regular-sized house door, at the rear of the building. It too was padlocked, but at least it was on the opposite end of the barn, and couldn't be viewed from Spencer's house.

Although I didn't have any tools, I did have some change in my pocket, another old habit firmly ingrained by my mother, who always asked me two things before I left the house: "Do you have to go to the bathroom?" and "Do you have money to make a phone call?" Mom thought of everything, and then some.

I pulled out a dime and unscrewed the strap hinges from the old, weathered door. It never ceases to amaze me that someone would take the trouble to padlock one side of a door, but use hinges that can be removed from the outside, as opposed to the more secure butt hinges, which are concealed on the interior door and jamb. A picklock would have worked too, but I had lost mine the last time I pulled off a B & E, and haven't gotten around to acquiring a new set.

Some of the screws were rusty, and their slits worn from years of tightening, so I had to file them with the sharp sides of the new dime for several minutes, before the impression was deep enough to accept my makeshift screwdriver. My fingers ached from the effort. It took what seemed like an hour to remove the six screws.

The door danced around in my hands when I opened it, using the padlock as a solitary hinge. I stepped inside the dark catacomb, greeted in the entryway by thick cobwebs that stuck to my face as I passed. I quickly let go of the concept that thousands of big, ugly, poisonous spiders were adhering to my entire body, ready to start biting in unison at the first human flesh to come through this entrance in a decade.

I pulled the door shut behind me as best I could, balancing it delicately on the dirt threshold. I wiped the spider webs from my face and neck, trying to convince myself that my thick jeans and jacket would protect me from creepy critters. My hair was my biggest concern, but the knit cap offered adequate defense, or so I tried to think.

It was as dark as a coalminer's armpit inside the barn, which smelled like mildewed alfalfa. I turned on my flashlight and took a quick survey. Concerned the light would send sporadic flashes through the cracks in the old, weathered single-wall construction of the building, I turned it off and paused in total darkness to allow myself a few deep breaths and a moment of profound satisfaction. When something amazing materializes before my eyes in a situation where any sound could jeopardize my safety, I have no recourse but to revel in silence.

An armored truck was the object engendering my nirvana-like state. I'd finally won a game, but screaming "Bingo!" at the top of my lungs was precluded, unless, like the black widow spider's mate, I welcomed death after reaching orgasmic heights.

There were a couple more pieces of business to tend to before I could leave. I turned on the flashlight again, just long enough to find my way to the driver's door, opened it and shined the light on the dashboard, in search of the small metal plate on which the serial number of the truck was stamped. It was there, in the far corner, up by the windshield. I had a ballpoint pen, but no paper, so I wrote the number on the palm of my hand. Next, I walked around to the back of the truck, and looked at the dual rear tires; sure enough, one was bald. Slowly, as quietly as a cat stalking a bird, I opened the back door of the truck and crawled in. Once inside the steel fortress, I could turn the flashlight on again, this time assured the light wouldn't show through the barn walls. Searching the back of the vehicle, I found the two guard's uniforms and a cap, identical to the one I'd found on the side of the road. My heart was racing so fast I had to pause again for a few more deep breaths; didn't want to blow it now, by freaking out or having a coronary in the back of the cold, dark metal monster. Calmed as much as I could get under the circumstances, I carefully backed out through the steel door.

Screwing the hinges back in place went much faster than dismantling them. Slowly and quietly, I made my way back to my car along the same route through the still forest. Once in it, and a few hundred yards back down Little Lake Road, I pulled into a turnout and released the tension I'd had to control so carefully in the musty old barn. I felt like I'd just hit a six-spot in a Keno machine, and elation that must be similar to what a burglar feels after pulling off a successful B & E. Sally Covington would have appreciated my triumph had she been along for the ride.

I drove back to Highway 1, pulled into Mendocino, and parked in front of the Seagull Inn to call Ed from the pay phone out in front. I asked him if he'd mind a late-night visitor; he said he'd love to see me. I jumped back in the car and drove the half dozen blocks to his house on the western edge of town.

There was a fine line regarding how much information I wanted to reveal to Ed about the data I'd collected the last few days. Sooner or later his boss was going to want to have a less-than-friendly chat with me about what I knew. The less Ed knew, I thought, the better off he'd be as far as his job security was concerned.

I decided not to tell him about tonight's foray.

"So what brings you out in the middle of the night?" Ed asked, as he opened the door to let me in.

"Just felt like a little human companionship before I head home to my furry roommate."

"C'mon in. I've got a warm fire going. You're sure bundled up, where've you been?"

I hated to lie to him. "Just a late walk out on the headlands, trying to piece together some of the more puzzling aspects of this mysterious quilt I seem to be working on.

I sat on the floor in front of the fireplace. Ed came over behind me and started to massage my shoulders. He realized at once his efforts were futile through the heavy wool coat, so he reached around, unbuttoned it, and slowly slid it off my shoulders and onto the floor. Then he continued, his strong hands rubbing my tired and aching shoulder muscles for a long time. Eventually I slid to the floor and lay on my stomach while he massaged my back, arms, legs, and neck as well as any masseur I'd ever been to.

During the entire hour of kneading and rubbing, neither of us spoke. I had entered some other state of consciousness, one of total relaxation, like nothing I could remember experiencing in recent history.

When he stopped, I looked up at him with sleepy, contented eyes. "You're awfully good at that. Remind me to return the favor sometime."

Ed stretched out on the floor beside me and pulled my turtleneck up over my head. "I have something else in mind," he said.

I was astounded by the passion I suddenly felt. It must have been because I was so relaxed, my mind void of all my worries, as blank as a sheet of notebook paper on the first day of class, leaving plenty of room for lustful notations and rotations. There was certainly a lot more tension to release than I had thought earlier, just after my scary, thrilling B & E.

Much later I told Ed I'd have to go home, even though it was about 2 a.m. Tank had to be fed, and I had things to do at home in the morning before going to the office—like changing out of my dark clothes.

Despite the hour, once home I couldn't fall asleep. On average, insomnia hits me twice a year. My relaxed state at Ed's dissipated once I hit the cold air and drove the winding road home, dodging several deer that sparked adrenalin through me, and once inside my cabin, I had to build a fire. All these activities, combined with the memory of my find in Spencer's barn, woke me thoroughly. Just what the hell did it mean? Was Spencer a big-time heroin dealer? Could it be that simple? Not likely. Most cases aren't solved so quickly and easily, and of course there was still Billy's death to consider. How did that connect to all of it?

My mind refused to cease-fire. Cat therapy sounded like the best move. I picked up Tank, carried him over to the bed, and switched on the TV at its foot. I found an old black-and-white movie, Fred Astaire and Ginger Rogers dancing across an elaborate stage. I leaned up against the pillows, snuggling Tank against my chest under the covers, much to his satisfaction, apparently, for he responded with a loud purr. The plot of the movie was thin, but the dancing superb.

CHAPTER 17

When I got to the office in the morning, I called a friend in Fort Bragg who works for the Department of Motor Vehicles and asked him to trace the serial number of the armored truck. He said he'd call me back later.

Then I called Ed, who said that Tony and Johnny were out on bail; a bondsman had sprung them early this morning. When he asked what I was doing for my evening's entertainment, I told him I had promised to play pinochle with friends. He made an exquisite attempt to entice me into a more appealing game, but I told him my promise to Lucia was irrevocable.

The phone rang just as I placed the receiver down.

"Syracuse?"

"Yes. Who is this?" I answered.

"Tony. I need your help," he said, sounding troubled.

"Sure, what can I do?"

"Me and Johnny need to take you up on your offer. We got nowhere to go, could we stay at your place?"

"Of course. Where are you now?"

"At a pay phone in Fort Bragg."

"Did a lawyer come to speak with you?"

"Yeah. She said we had a good chance of getting off easy, since it was the first time we've ever been in trouble."

"Good. Now listen, it's a little tricky to find my cabin, so I better come in and meet you. Is there a safe place close by you could go to until I get there, say in fifteen minutes?"

"We're not far from the movie theater. How about there?"

"Okay. I'll be right there," I said, hanging up the receiver.

My cabin was too small; why the hell had I promised the boys they could stay there? Because I needed their testimony and they needed protection. Whomever they'd ripped off was probably madder than a rabid skunk. Maybe Ed would be willing to trade off with me, but then I'd have to tell him why these guys were so important to me.

When I descended the stairs, Lucia yelled out the front door not to forget about our pinochle game with Harriet and Larry; she'd meet me at the store at six o'clock, and we'd go out to their house for dinner and cards. I gave her a thumbs-up and stepped into my Volvo.

The drive took twenty minutes. I found a parking place in the lot adjoining the theater. Tony and Johnny were nowhere in sight, so I assumed they had gone into the movie house, which also has a video store off the lobby. I guessed they were perusing movie titles while they waited for me.

After searching the aisles, I asked the clerk if she'd seen two young guys—probably in jeans and flannel shirts—near the theater in the last few minutes. She said they'd come in, but entered the theater lobby to use the restroom. I waited by the counter. After five more minutes passed and they still hadn't come out, I walked into the lobby and reluctantly entered the men's room—reluctantly, because that's how I'd met my ex-husband, using a men's room in a saloon in Tempe, Arizona, when my beer-filled bladder couldn't wait for the women's room to be vacated. Noticing my dainty little feet in the cubicle beside him, he said, "Any woman sassy enough to use a men's room is worth buying a drink for." The rest is history.

I stayed in the vicinity of the theater for over an hour. I

walked around the block, cruised the video aisles, inspected all the exits, looked in all three of the theater's screening rooms, and checked the men's room once again. Tony and Johnny had vanished. There was nothing to do but return to my office and hope they'd call.

Unfortunately, there was no message from them when I got back, so I called Ed. I asked him who had put up bail for the boys, and he gave me the name of a local bondsman, whom I rang up next. Pleading confidentiality, he refused to reveal who'd hired him. I knew I could probably get a court order to extract the information from the son-of-a-bitch, but that wasn't going to help me this instant.

My answering machine did offer word from my friend at the DMV, so I called him next. The truck was registered to Unlimited Productions Company in Los Angeles, and had been purchased through an L.A. auction yard called Lasher's. After calling information to get that number, I placed the call and was greeted by a pleasant receptionist who was more than happy to look up the sale in her records, refreshing after all the brick walls I'd run up against until now. She could only repeat what my friend at the DMV said, so I asked if she had a record of which salesperson had filled out the papers. I was put on hold and tortured by elevator music for several minutes, before a man's voice came on the line. I explained that I was a bookkeeper with Unlimited Productions, and we had some questions concerning the purchase of the truck for our records, since we'd misplaced the purchase order for the vehicle and no one knew where the validation papers were or who contracted the sale.

The man said he had only a faint recollection of the sale, wouldn't ordinarily have any memory of it at all due to the tremendous volume of business they did, but since it was an unusual truck he vaguely remembered the transaction, but not the name of the individual who signed the sales contract. He was only able to recall the buyer as an older man, maybe fifties or sixties, and as good looking as every Hollywood type that came through his door. I thanked him and hung up.

My mind felt as strained as pureed baby food. My ear was numb from the series of phone calls, but I had more to make. I switched ears and dialed Harriet's number.

"Hello, yes," she answered.

"Harriet, it's Syracuse. Got a small favor to ask if you've got a sec."

"Sure. What can I do for you?"

"Don't you have some kind of directory that lists the names of all the production companies?"

"Yes, of course. It's one of the main tools of the trade."

"Could you look up Unlimited Productions Company for me?"

She asked me to hold the line for a minute while she went to her bookcase to look it up. If this was what it was like to be a telephone operator, with one ear affixed to a receiver all day, I began to have great empathy for Ma Bell's employees. I switched ears again, swallowed the last of the coffee I'd picked up at the bakery on my way to the office, and leaned back against my chair to wait.

"Not here, Syracuse, no such listing," Harriet said, when she finally returned to the phone.

"What does that mean?" I asked.

"My directory is up to date, so they could either be very new in the business or a bogus outfit. You could check to see if they published a fictitious-name statement with any of a zillion Los Angeles area newspapers, or you could call all the county clerks in Southern California who would have the notices on file. Depends on how crazy you want to make yourself."

"Yeah, well, I don't know what I'm going to do, but I'll see you tonight for dinner and cards. Maybe I'll have discovered something by then."

"Sure. Ciao."

I decided I couldn't bear the thought of calling every newspaper and county clerk in greater Los Angeles this afternoon. It was four o'clock and I was tired. Instead of subjecting myself to the tedious calls, I opted for a stroll on the headlands to clear my brain with fresh, ocean air. My poor mind was beginning to feel like scrambled eggs prepared by an overzealous novice chef.

I didn't return to my office until six o'clock, just in time to meet Lucia for our dinner and pinochle date. The walk along the cliffs, combined with the refreshing sea breezes, had revived me, and I was in the mood for a hearty dinner and challenging card game. Lucia and I have been playing partner pinochle against Harriet and Larry for years. I knew it would be the perfect respite after the disconcerting day I'd had. There was still no word from Tony and Johnny, so I left an outgoing message on my answering machine for any incoming calls to be forwarded to Harriet's number. I didn't want to miss the boys' call—and I sure as hell wondered where they were.

(HAPTER 18

After a pun-filled evening with my pinochle gang, Larry excelling as usual with a plentiful array of plays on words during the action-packed, best-two-out-of-three series (which Lucia and I won), I returned to my cabin at about 2 a.m.

I'd forgotten to leave an outside light on, and it was as dark as the two queens of spades earlier tonight, when, much to Harriet and Larry's chagrin, Lucia produced a double pinochle. I fished around the bottom of my purse for my flashlight, felt a sharp pain in my back, couldn't believe I'd pulled a muscle performing such an innocuous maneuver, and apparently slumped into unconsciousness.

I must have been out for the long count, because the next thing I remembered was a blindingly bright searchlight. The light subsided when I fluttered my eyelids and tried to shield my eyes with a hand that felt like it was encased in lead. I looked at my surroundings in an effort to ascertain where I was. Lying on a bed flanked by a nurse in a starched white uniform, and a doctor in matching white medical jacket, indicated rather strongly I must be in a hospital. Further scrutiny revealed Ed and Lucia standing quietly at the foot of my bed.

My face must have revealed my perplexity, for the physician, apparently sensing my bewilderment, spoke up. "Syracuse, you're going to be fine. You're in the Coast Hospital. You caught a bullet in your back, but fortunately it missed all your vital organs," he announced, in the soft, reassuring voice seasoned doctors use, whether preparing you for the deep six or telling you it's benign. "You do have a chipped rib, a mild concussion and some sore muscles, and you'll have to stay with us for a couple of days so we can keep an eye on you," he added. "You can visit her for ten minutes, but then I want her to get some more rest," he said, addressing his comment to the foot of the bed.

"How long have I been here?" I asked.

"You didn't show up at your office this morning and didn't answer your phone, so I drove out to your place, because I had a feeling something like this was going to happen sooner or later, even though you think you're Superwoman," Lucia answered. "That bump on your head must have happened when you fell and got knocked out cold."

"You're lucky you didn't bleed to death during the night; the doctor said it was a fluke the bullet didn't hit anything that'd cause a lot of bleeding," Ed piped in.

"Don't tell her that, Ed, or she'll really believe she's some kind of supernatural sleuth," Lucia added, in her usual candid style.

"Lucia, how's my Tank?"

"Pissed, but full. I gave him some extra food and a treat. I'll go back out tonight, before it gets dark, I might add, in case your gun-happy friend decides to come out for another crack at you, and to be sure Tank has plenty of food to hold him over. He's so goddamn fat, he could probably live without food for a month, just surviving on his excess corpulence."

"Did you get a look at the slug, Ed?"

"Yeah. A twenty-two."

"Probably a rifle from a distance, don't you think?" I mumbled. I was beginning to feel sleepy again; it was an effort to keep my eyes open.

"Yeah. Now listen, you're going to have to stick around here for a couple of days. I'll stay with you when I'm off duty, and see if I can get some other deputies to stand watch while I'm at the office. Don't want this semi-sharpshooter to have another shot," Ed said.

"And I'm going out to buy you some new clothes—like a bulletproof vest, if I can find something that exotic in Fort Bragg," Lucia quipped.

Once again I lapsed into sound sleep, and didn't awaken until the phone on the bedside table rang several hours later. At first I had no idea where I was, but the hospital smells alerted me before my other senses had a chance to catch up. Reaching for the receiver, I groaned in pain. I'd always heard that ribs hurt a lot if you chipped or broke them—now I believed it.

On the other end of the line was my daughter, calling from Humboldt State University, up near Eureka. Lucia had just called to tell her what happened, and she wanted to come to the hospital, which is a good three-hour drive from the school, but she was in the middle of final exams and didn't know what to do.

I explained to her that my injuries were band-aid material; I was getting out of this joint tomorrow, and was just fine, in case she couldn't sense that from my irritable mood. Even though I appreciated her concern, I was also equally affected by the billions of dollars I've invested in her college education, and wasn't going to have her blow her final exams over one chipped rib and a knot on my head. She said she'd be down for Christmas vacation in a week and would see me then.

My strength waned again, a combination, I guessed, of my injuries and the medication I was taking. I fell asleep and didn't wake up until a nurse brought in a breakfast tray the following morning. I'd missed Ed's nocturnal visit entirely; he'd already left for work. I could see he had used a cot set up next to my bed, but must have arrived and left quietly, since I hadn't stirred once during the night.

When I tried to sit up to sip the hot tea, the pain felt like someone was twisting a knife in my back. On hearing me groan, the nurse explained that injured ribs are generally sore for quite awhile.

"Wait till the first time you sneeze, honey, that really jolts them hard," she said, trying to humor me, but not succeeding. She gave me a pain pill, which I accepted gratefully and swallowed with a paper cup full of watered-down orange juice.

Through the open door, I spotted a day-shift deputy stationed in the hall. He sat in a folding chair, reading a paperback. I wondered if the sheriff's department would so willingly offer this kind of protection to just anyone, or if Ed's influence was responsible for the additional security.

Lucia strolled through the door early, arms burdened with a stack of magazines and a bouquet of silver roses—my favorite. Their aroma quickly filled the room, helping mask the odor of alcohol and other antiseptic hospital smells, and perking up my somber mood. I had drifted into feeling sorry for myself, hating the idea of being temporarily incarcerated, even if my sentence was of short duration. I felt like a caged animal in a human zoo.

She walked over to the side of my bed, gave me a peck on the cheek, and sat down on Ed's cot. I said, "You can imagine how much I relish being in here."

"I know. You can't miss a day of detecting, even if someone tries to kill you for it," she said, her tone sarcastic.

"I'm sure you wouldn't do any better in here. I know you're terrified of needles; it takes three nurses just for a simple blood test, because two of them have to sit on you."

"You're right, my little private detective, but I wasn't the bull's eye on this caper, you were, and this is the best and safest place you can be until you get your strength back."

"Yeah, well that doesn't mean I have to like it. I'm getting out of here tomorrow," I announced emphatically, but once again felt myself drifting off to slumberland.

Around six that evening I woke to the sound of Ed's voice. He'd stopped by to spend the night and had brought me some food from the outside world, expecting it would lift my spirits as well as my appetite.

With much moaning and groaning I pulled myself up to a sitting position and asked, "Can I assume the department is looking into this?"

He lowered his head. "Yeah, but there's a lot more to it now."

"Whaddya mean?"

Ed came to the side of my bed and put both of his large, strong hands around mine. He looked softly into my eyes and made an effort to smile, but couldn't. *Christ, what the hell is going on now?*

"I'm sorry, Syracuse, but our marksman was one busy fellow this week. I'm afraid Tony and Johnny didn't fare as well as you did: some fishermen down at Noyo Harbor discovered both of them this morning; their bodies washed up on shore, both with several well-placed bullets in them."

I leaned my hand against my cheek and twisted my mouth. "Damn! I knew something had happened to them." I told Ed about their call and my inability to find them at the theater. "I guess I don't have to ask if they were twenty-twos."

"Yeah, they were. Ballistics hasn't matched them yet, but I'd bet my season tickets to the Giants' games they will."

"I wouldn't get that extreme, Ed," I kidded, but this was upsetting news. I needed the boys' testimony. I looked up at Ed and said, "I'm getting out of here tomorrow. Could you do me a couple of favors?"

"Sure," he said, without hesitation, "But only if you'll level with me. I want to know what Tony and Johnny told you that day you came to the office, because they didn't blab a word to anyone else as far I can tell."

"It's your ass, Ed, if I do."

"I'm willing to take the chance, baby. This case of yours is getting out of your league, if you ask me."

"I don't think so, but here goes, anyway." I proceeded to tell Ed everything about the boys and the case up until now. When I'd finished my story he shook his head, puzzled by the turn of events.

"For once, I don't even know what to say, but I'll keep your secrets until the department finds out for itself, and then start looking for a new job. What was the favor you wanted?"

"Go to my office. I'll give you the combination to my safe. My gun's in there, and I want it before I leave the hospital. Maybe you could pick it up in the morning before you go to work. There's a box of ammo and a holster too. Bring all of it."

"Anything else?"

"I was going to ask you to pick up a bullet-proof vest if there's an extra one lying around your office. Ordinarily I wouldn't dream of using one, but with this sore rib and my aching muscles, I can't move or duck very fast, so I think I might need the added protection for a few days." He nodded his head in agreement.

After nibbling on some of the food Ed had brought, including a tasty chocolate milk shake, we played a few rounds of gin rummy. Either I was too drugged, or he excelled at cards, because he trounced me.

CHAPTER 19

Ed slipped out early the next morning, and returned just as I was eating breakfast, which consisted of runny eggs, soggy toast, and weak coffee. To think they actually pay nutritionists at these joints, and this is all they can come up with, for crying out loud.

In addition to my gun and a vest, Ed brought a change of clothes Lucia had picked out for me, and a heavy jacket to conceal the vest and holster. He had to get back to his office, but we smooched for a few minutes, proving my blood was still able to circulate to all the more important parts of my wounded body.

While I was going through the strenuous and painful motions of getting dressed, Lucia called to say she'd be by in about fifteen minutes to take me to my cabin and my awaiting car. I thanked her for her thoughtfulness. The idea of a bus ride in my condition wasn't very appealing, and we don't have cabs in this rural part of the state.

An orderly pushing a wheelchair entered the room to escort me to the front door. Hospital procedure, he explained, knowing full well I was capable of walking on my own two feet to the exit. Covering their sweet asses was what they were doing, in case I fell down and killed myself on the perennially highly waxed tile floor, on which even a perfectly healthy person had to walk gingerly.

The sheriff's deputy assigned to me remained at my side until Lucia pulled up in front. I didn't recognize her car. She had to wave and honk to get my attention; she was behind the wheel of a new silver Mercedes and grinning from earring to earring. The orderly wheeled me to the car door and opened it. I slid carefully into the luxurious new automobile, a perplexed look on my face, and said, "You didn't tell me you were getting this!"

"You know I've been looking for the perfect car for months now. I read about this in an ad in the *Ukiah Daily Journal*. Yesterday, I decided to drive there in my old car to check it out, and on the way over the hill my clutch went out. After spending hours with tow-truck drivers and mechanics, I decided fate had stepped in and told me to buy this, so I did. What do you think?"

"I'm still in shock. It's beautiful. Where's the old car?"

"Still in Ukiah. I have to wait until it's repaired before I can pick it up and then try to sell it over here." Excitement in her voice, she added, "Besides, this rides like a dream, and I thought you'd appreciate a gentle voyage for that sore rib of yours."

As we drove along the coast, I looked out at the ocean and the white waves crashing against the cliffs. A few surfers in wet suits braved the cold water. Lucia kept up a running monologue, proudly pointing out to me what the hundreds of buttons and switches on the instrument panel were for. Trying to look enthused, I reached into the glove box several times to look things up in the owner's manual, but I was secretly maintaining my unwavering dedication to Volvos.

It took about half an hour to reach my cabin. As we walked up to it, Lucia said, "Aren't you a little afraid to be here? You know, back at the scene of the crime. Isn't that where the bad guys return to, especially if they missed their target the first time around?"

"Not as long as you're with me. You're my witness, sweetheart,"

I said, accenting *sweetheart* with my best Bogart impression.

"Well, it gives me the creeps. Someone must have followed you to Harriet and Larry's, and then back here. Thank God they had a shitty aim."

"It was pitch black outside. They probably couldn't see me well enough to get off an accurate pop," I said, confidently.

"Still, I'd feel better if you'd stay at my place for a few days, at least until they catch whoever did it," she pleaded.

"What about His Tankness?" I said, just as Tank sauntered over and began rubbing his head against my leg.

"Maybe the woman across the road could feed him, or someone could come out here with you whenever you have to. I'd just feel better, and would definitely sleep better, if you were at my place. There's plenty of room."

Feeling her concern, and mine as well, I decided to agree. "You're probably right." I called my neighbor, who said she'd be more than happy to take care of Tank. I didn't explain to her what was going on, just that I'd be out of town for a few days, and would be in touch with her. To preclude having to worry about the sniper accidentally taking a shot at her, I asked her to do the evening feeding before dark, saying that Tank expected it then.

After packing a small suitcase and giving Tank a final roughing up, Lucia and I headed to our cars. She had to get back to her store, and I had some detecting to do.

I turned north and drove straight for Anne's, my rib aching every time I shifted gears or turned the wheel.

The blue Mercedes was parked in front of Anne's house when I pulled up in the circular driveway. I nuzzled up next to it, slowly and painfully disembarked from my vehicle, and made my way toward the front door, which Anne opened before I'd had a chance to ring the bell. She must have heard me drive up in the quiet of the forest sanctuary.

"Hi, Syracuse. What brings you out here?" she said.

"More to talk about. May I come in?"

"Of course," she said, pointing the way to the lavish art deco living room we had previously visited in.

"Where's Roger?" I asked.

"Unexpected business, as usual. He had to go down to Mexico for a few days."

As soon as we were seated on the familiar leather chairs, I began: "I'm going to make a very long and harrowing story short. Someone took a shot at me a couple of nights ago, and at the same time killed the two boys I'd found who were involved in the armored truck heist."

Anne's blue eyes were like magnets holding my gaze. Then she stood, went over to the window, and looked out for a few moments without speaking. When she looked back at me there was shock and utter disbelief on her lovely face.

"I hardly know what to say. I'm so sorry about this. Were you hurt?"

"Just a chipped rib and a bump on my head. Hurts some, but I'm managing," I lied. Hurt like hell was more like it.

"Do you have any idea who did it?"

"Yes and no. The sheriff is investigating, and he might be able to trace the gun, I don't know. I'm still pretty exhausted from the wound, so I can only do a minimum of work until I get my strength back."

"Well, thank God you're all right," she said.

Though I'd rehearsed my next few sentences 100 times, I still hadn't come up with a gentle way to divulge my theory to her. I knew, no matter how I phrased it, that it was still going to come out the same way—a way that would upset her.

"Anne, I'm not sure how to tell you this, but I have to." I squirmed in my chair, and then added, "I suspect your father has something to do with all of this."

"You can't be serious! Why would you say that?" Anne said, appalled, exactly as I thought she would be.

"For starters, the armored truck you saw, the one that turned out to have heroin in it, is parked in the red barn in your father's pasture."

At this news, Anne walked to one of the leather couches and sat down in complete silence. She looked hurt and bewildered. I slid over next to her and placed my hand on hers. She began to shake her head in disbelief.

"My father would never hurt, much less kill, anyone," she said, softly.

"Maybe he hired someone to do it?" I offered.

"No. No, he's not that kind of person. He really isn't," she said, in such a convincing tone that I began to doubt my own conclusion, but nonetheless continued the onslaught.

"Then what in the hell is that truck doing out in the barn?"

"I have no idea. I didn't know it was there."

Diplomacy was my intention with Anne, but the combination of delicate circumstances and the blatant facts unfolding in this case required me to be forceful yet considerate, as if the two could run concurrently. Taking a deep breath, which, rather than relieving the tension I felt, only wrenched my jagged rib further into my side, I plunged ahead. "Is there any chance Roger is responsible for the truck?"

It felt like Anne's blue eyes were piercing my brain, as if she were attempting to discern how I could possibly question the integrity of the two main men in her life.

"Roger is an honest and decent man. He couldn't be involved in this any more than Father could. Quite frankly, Syracuse, I'm perplexed by your accusations, because I know both of them so well, much better then you ever could, and I'm sure neither of them is implicated in this, despite the fact that the truck is parked out there. All I can think of is, perhaps someone planted it there to put the blame on Father or Roger. What do you think?" she pleaded.

"I have to admit I hadn't considered that. We could find out easily enough, though, by asking them if they know about it.

When will Roger be back? And where is your father?"

Her eyes brightened at this new possibility. "Roger will be back tomorrow. Father should be home tonight around five."

"Here's the approach I'd like to take: please don't talk to your father about this; leave that to me. I'll come out here about five-thirty and we can discuss it with him together. How's that sound?"

"Fine."

She stood, and walked me to the door. I was exhausted from the visit, but probably would have felt equally tired if I were home, horizontal, with a fat cat on my chest. I apologized to Anne for any discomfort I'd caused her, and said I'd see her in a few hours. I drove back to the office, curled up on the couch, and fell fast asleep for the rest of the afternoon.

CHAPTER 20

I awoke to the sound of my phone ringing. Sure at first that it was the alarm clock, I groped around in search of the incessant chime. Once I figured out I was in my office, I got up and went to the phone. It was Lucia. I told her I had taken an extended catnap and was leaving soon to go out to meet Anne, but I would meet her at her house as soon as I was finished, probably around seven. She said she'd have dinner waiting when I arrived.

It was four-thirty. My side was aching more than when I'd fallen asleep. Not wanting to take any more prescription pain-killers, I swallowed two aspirin from the medicine chest in the small bathroom adjacent to the office. Then I ran a brush through my hair, put the bullet-proof vest back on, attached my shoulder holster, stuck my loaded thirty-eight in it, and pulled on a heavy down jacket.

I stopped in the Mendocino Bakery for a sweet Danish with slivered almonds and a strong cup of coffee. Sugar and caffeine power was my best hope during this infirmity. It was no easy task walking around with a knife in my back that twisted with every move I made. I felt like my veins had been emptied of blood, then refilled with lead.

I walked slowly out to my Volvo, which offered security as

strong as my bulletproof vest. For the past twenty years I'd recommended Volvos to all my friends, saying they were the safest cars on the road. I've owned four, and even keep my daughter supplied with a decent one at all times. If you're going to be in an accident, there's no point being the first one there, which is the case with most of the mass-produced aluminum cans that pass for cars today. Assuming my daughter was safely encased in her Volvo, I wasn't thrilled to learn that her latest boyfriend drives a Volkswagen van!

The drive to Anne's had become so familiar that I felt like an old horse instinctively returning to the barn, only the barn in this case wasn't being used for equestrian purposes. I arrived at five-twenty. The only car in the driveway was Anne's blue Mercedes. She answered my knock immediately. Just as I stepped across the threshold, Frank Spencer pulled up in front of his house. Anne waved for him to come over. I wasn't sure if he had recognized me yet, so I quickly stepped into the foyer.

"Hi, honey," Spencer said, as he entered the room; then, spotting me, his expression swiftly changed from warm father to cold prick.

"Mr. Spencer, before you fly off the handle, please hear me out, and I promise I'll never darken your doorstep again," I said, meaning it, in the most polite voice I could muster for the occasion. "I must speak with you," I added. "It's most urgent."

"O.K., I'll give you five minutes. Let's go over to my study," he said, spinning on his heel. Anne and I followed him in silence.

If I thought Anne's home was the epitome of *Better Homes and Gardens*, Spencer's fell more into the Taj Mahal category. The furnishings defied description from my limited but somewhat knowledgeable lexicon of architectural terms. Spencer led us down a hallway to his study at the southeast corner of the mansion. Floor-to-ceiling oak bookcases housed more volumes than Fort Bragg's public library. A Persian carpet, silk I'm sure, and worth more than all my worldly goods, was centered in the middle of an immaculate, glistening hardwood floor. Spencer's green-leather-topped desk was enormous. *Bankers don't make this kind of dough. There's got to be some family money here, or other sources of income, like heroin profits, to keep this guy in such plush surroundings.*

Spencer seated himself behind his desk; Anne and I sat facing him, in straight-backed oak chairs. Preparing myself for the interrogation I was about to begin, I silently recited part of "Our Father" in an attempt to calm my nerves, sensing I was going to need all the help I could get while verbally pummeling this guy. Ed would be furious at me for confronting Spencer alone, but I was in one of my "don't give a shit" moods at this point.

Spencer spoke first, his voice sounding like he was struggling to control his annoyance. "What do you want with my family and me *now?* " he said coldly.

I decided to be tactful, because coming on hostile or menacing at this point would be about as smart as cooking bacon while naked. I already had enough scars from this case. I loosened my jacket before I spoke, to be certain my gun was in easy reach.

"Mr. Spencer, believe me, I really don't want to keep badgering you, but I have a few questions that only you can answer. If you're not willing to assist me, I can assure you I'll have no difficulty getting a subpoena for you to appear in court to tell the entire world what you know about this case.

"Some time ago I talked with the two men who robbed the armored truck Anne saw on Little Lake Road. They were arrested for selling heroin, and after they were released on bail, both were murdered. The same sniper took a shot at me, but I sustained only minor injuries. I suspect the same person killed your son, using a hypodermic needle instead of a rifle. Now, the biggest question in my mind is, why is the armored truck that was used in this caper, and which was carrying heroin, by the way, not money, why is that very truck hidden in your red barn?" I said, pointing out the window toward his pasture.

"I don't know anything about it," he said.

"I told you, Syracuse," Anne piped in.

Ignoring her, I said, "I think you do," in as firm a tone as I could muster.

Looking lost in thought, Spencer rubbed his fingertips across his forehead. Assured and vital just moments before, he suddenly seemed tired and vulnerable. For a moment he looked away from me and peered out the window at the barn beyond. When he turned back to me, I could feel the change in him: he appeared about as stable as a house of cards. I began to feel a surge of impatience, but was willing to give him a chance to compose himself, though I didn't think he deserved it. Anne sat, quiet and motionless, beside me.

"My son has been killed. Elizabeth, Elizabeth..." he stammered, unable to finish the sentence. He buried his face in his hands and slumped over his desk, crumbling from the inner turmoil he must have felt. Then he reached over to the upper right-hand drawer of his desk and slowly withdrew a revolver.

I spoke quickly: "Mr. Spencer, please don't make this worse than it already is. Your daughter is sitting right here with us, please don't distress her any more," I said in a soft tone, as if addressing a child. I knew my bulletproof vest had its limitations, and at the same time couldn't imagine Spencer would shoot me in front of Anne. It was one of the reasons I'd had her come along for this summit meeting.

"Father, everything is going to be all right. Please put the gun down. Syracuse can help you," she pleaded.

Spencer raised the revolver before I could reach for mine. In one quick motion, I pushed Anne to the floor and rolled away from my sitting position onto the rug next to her. I peeked up at Spencer briefly as I drew my gun and aimed it at his face. He turned the muzzle of his revolver, placed it against his right temple, and fired; his brains spilled onto the leather desktop.

Anne was still face down on the floor. I told her to get up, turn, and leave the room without looking at her father. She obeyed. We stepped out to the hallway, then walked back to her house, where I called Ed as soon as I had Anne settled on the couch.

After Ed and a host of deputies arrived to do their part, I instructed Anne to pack a bag, intending for her to spend the night with Lucia and me, since Roger wouldn't be back until tomorrow and I wouldn't leave her there alone.

She offered no resistance. A sob cracked her deep voice. "This is all a nightmare, Syracuse. Tell me I'm going to wake up and it's all going to be over," she muttered.

"I wish I could. C'mon, let's go. We can piece some of this together tonight at Lucia's."

We went over the case for hours. Ed joined us, adding his input, which included nothing new from the sheriff's department. They still had no leads on the sniper, and Frank Spencer's suicide didn't offer any concrete information, either. It seemed to comfort Anne to go over all the material, to somehow help her begin to cope with the ghastly situation.

My strength pushed beyond its limits, I had to retire before Lucia and Anne did. Remarking that she seemed to be running a bed and breakfast inn tonight, Lucia asked if Ed wanted to stay over too, but he said he had things to do at home that couldn't wait. I left them all still talking, while I slipped off into the guest room. Snuggled between soft, rose-colored flannel sheets, I fell asleep immediately, too exhausted to spend another moment mulling over the latest developments in the perplexing case.

CHAPTER 21

Lucia and Anne were drinking tea and eating toast at the dining room table when I crawled into the kitchen the following morning. I felt like I'd been drugged with Elizabeth's Seconal, and couldn't shake the aftereffects. The fog rolling in from the coast echoed the condition of my mind as I glanced out the window. I headed straight for the coffee pot.

"Might have to do this stuff intravenously this morning," I remarked to the two of them, who looked like they'd struck up an immediate friendship. Lucia excelled in a crisis, and I suspected she knew all the right things to say to Anne. She could do a much better job of consoling Anne than I could, and they'd probably stayed up half the night, with Lucia offering a comforting shoulder for Anne to unload the awful burden of her father's sudden, violent death. The current topic, however, was clothing, and the possibility of Anne's coming down to Lucia's store to look over a newly arrived line with an Ivy League emphasis.

"Roger called my machine from the airport this morning and got this number. He should be here any time to pick me up," Anne said.

"Good. I'd like to talk with him," I responded sluggishly, "but first this coffee has to work, or I'll be of slightly diminished capacity as an investigator today."

Lucia had left this morning's *San Francisco Chronicle* on the coffee table, so I plopped down on the inviting couch to read the business section, so I could see how much more my stock, which had been declining steadily for weeks, had dropped in the past few days. The shock of the crashing Dow might work better than java on my logy central nervous system. I was right: the stock had fallen another full point. Damn, I sure knew how to pick them. Rather than clear my stupor, the stock's continued plunge only made me angry with myself for not investing the money in real estate, but no, I'd had some ridiculous hunch that running shoes would soar this year, with all the health consciousness around jogging, and the famous athletes endorsing my favorite brand.

Lucia spoke, breaking my trance: "We stayed up most of the night, Syracuse. Turns out Anne is from Virginia too, so we talked about growing up there, and then tried to be detectives for a while, but I'm sure we didn't come up with anything more than you already have."

I rested a hand on top of my head and stared at the rose-colored carpeting. If Spencer was the ringleader of this entire heroin circus, then the case had come to a close as far as I was concerned. There were still a few loose ends, like locating the twenty-two that had been used on the boys and me. I'm sure the sheriff was combing Spencer's home, so I made a note to call Ed and ask him what, if anything, they'd found out there.

It was becoming increasingly difficult to question Anne. With the loss of her father added to her already overburdened mind, I didn't know how to begin, but decided to plunge right back into the muddy waters with her, even if it meant stirring up more sludge from the bottom.

Both Anne and Lucia had joined me in the living room, sitting next to one another on a smaller couch on my left. I looked at Anne with what I hoped appeared to be a concerned, solemn face when I spoke.

"Anne, I'm sure you must agree at this point that your father—and please excuse me if it seems absurdly self-evident to suggest this—was at the very least a deeply troubled man. I think he was concealing something related to this whole armored truck mess. The problem is, I don't know just what." I didn't want to add I that also assumed he was the head honcho, feeling I'd already said enough to upset her.

"I'm as puzzled as you are," Anne responded.

At the sound of the toaster popping, Lucia got up and brought me a plate of corn bread toast with a thin layer of honey on it. "I'm sure Sam Spade would prefer bourbon and water, but I think this honey will do the trick even better in your situation. How's the rib feel this morning?"

"Still sore as hell; my acrobatics yesterday didn't help any."

She turned to Anne and asked, "Is there anything I can bring you from the kitchen? More tea?"

"No. No, thank you," Anne replied.

"Anne, I don't know where I'm going from here with this case. At this point it looks like the sheriff's department is at least as involved as I am. They'll be out at your father's today, going over the whole place with a fine-toothed comb. I'll wait and see what they come up with, and maybe we'll have some concrete results in the next day or two. I agree with you in not believing your father would kill anyone, and I don't think he was the one who shot at me. Call it instinct; until we know for sure, I'm going to continue to stay here at Lucia's, so if you need to reach me, you should phone me here, but please don't tell anyone this is where I'm hiding out, not even anyone as innocuous as the gardener, because, frankly, I don't know whom to suspect of what right now, and I'm quickly losing trust for much of the human race."

There was a knock at the front door, and Lucia walked across the room to open it. Roger Phelps stood in the entry hall, his face anguished and concerned. He removed his hat and went to

Anne, taking her into his outstretched arms. "I'm so sorry, dear, so sorry," he said, gently and reassuringly. Lucia and I took this as our cue to leave the two of them alone for a bit, while we moved into the kitchen and busied ourselves doing the dishes.

After a respectable interval, I returned to the living room and sat across from Anne and Roger, on the same couch I'd used earlier. I brought another cup of coffee along, feeling the need for one more shot of caffeine. Lucia followed with a tray of tea and toast for Roger, which he accepted politely.

"I realize this is a difficult time, Roger, but I have a few questions to ask you, and I have to move quickly on this, because we might still have a sniper out there with a smoking gun and an itchy trigger finger."

Anne had told Roger everything that had transpired to date, including the events leading up to Spencer's suicide.

Getting right to the point, I asked, "What do you know about the armored truck in the barn?" I checked his reaction, but couldn't read anything into his blank stare.

"I didn't know it was there," he answered softly. "I never walk over there, haven't any reason to," he added. His eyes focusing on mine, I could sense he was as perplexed as were the rest of us.

"What about Spencer's behavior in the past few weeks? Did you notice anything different about him or his activities?"

Roger looked at Anne, then turned his attention back to me. "He did seem more irritable than usual, but I assumed it was the stress from Elizabeth's hospitalization and Billy's death."

"But doesn't it seem to you he must have known something, or been involved in some way with this truck? I mean, the truck was in his barn, for crying out loud."

"Well, yes, it does appear that way on the surface, but I've known Frank for years, and I can't imagine him being involved in anything criminal," he said, stressing *criminal* as though it were a concept foreign to his apparently moral and affluent lifestyle.

I tried another approach: "A new theory I've been postulating, one that Anne actually brought up, is that perhaps the truck was planted by someone else; maybe someone was blackmailing Frank."

"Hmm, that's a thought," Roger said, sipping his tea.

"Maybe after all these years, someone came to Frank with the knowledge of who Billy's actual father was, or maybe the real father himself appeared. Do you have any idea who he might be?" I asked optimistically

Both Anne and Roger's faces brightened at this prospect, but neither of them knew the identity of Billy's real father. Elizabeth would, of course, but she was in no shape to question.

I continued this new train of thought. "Have any strangers been to his house lately?"

Roger answered for them. "That's really hard to say; we haven't lived here very long, so almost everyone is a stranger to us." I had to agree with him.

Lucia brought us more coffee and tea, although my bladder was on full. I excused myself to use the bathroom. Alone in there, I decided I had nothing more to ask the two of them, but did have some things to check out on my own. When I returned to the room, I told them they could go, asking them to call me if they thought of anything at all that might help. Anne and Lucia exchanged warm pleasantries before Anne left; I too gave her a hug and offered additional condolences on her father's death. Roger and I shook hands, and he thanked Lucia for the tea and toast.

After they left, I stretched out on the couch and turned on the TV with the remote control on the end table. A morning talk show blared, an interview with transvestites and their natural parents.

"Don't you have to go to work, Lucia?" I asked, peering up from my horizontal position on the comfy couch.

"Don't you, Sherlock?" she retorted.

"I think I'd rather be a housewife for the day: watch the tube, eat chocolate, and try to regain some of my super powers," I quipped.

"Make yourself at home, but you'll eventually have at least five cats perched on you—you're in a perfect position to become a cat mattress, and they'll be in any minute now from their morning walks. At least they only weigh half what your Tank does."

"I'm just going to hang out awhile; I'll come into the office this afternoon."

"O.K., see you then," she said, going out the door.

The TV program failed to hold my interest, even though the subject matter was intriguing. My inquiring mind was too absorbed in trying to figure out what Spencer had been up to, and why it was so painful that he'd had to ruin his costly Persian carpet with bloodstains that would never come out.

I called Ed, who said a swarm of deputies were out at Spencer's place, but so far no sign of a twenty-two. Spencer's revolver was a thirty-eight.

I took a long shower, soaking in the warmth until the hot water heater was depleted. I believe in water conservation, but felt I could allow this environmental inconsistency just for once due to my pained condition. I rubbed balm on my side, swallowed two aspirin with a glass of half-and-half to soothe my ever-present ulcer, then slowly dressed in my suit of armor and slung my thirty-eight over my shoulder.

Mendocino was packed with tourists who were descending on it for the Christmas holidays. I stepped into the Gallery Bookshop and picked up half a dozen books for various friends, thinking it'd be smart to chip away at my Christmas list while I had a few minutes to shop. It looked like the crowds would only intensify, and my irritability level would peak if I waited till Christmas Eve to try to do it all.

I bought my daughter a book on how to write term papers, which she frequently asked me to edit, and Lucia two mysteries by one of her favorite authors. For Ed, I chose a cookbook and a photography book, because he said he was going to start taking photography seriously this year, and maybe even have his own show at one of the local galleries; I hoped the cookbook would inspire him in several ways.

Next, I drove to Ed's house, made enlargements of the funeral photos, picked up my negatives and contact sheet, and took the blow-ups over to the local print shop, which faxed them to the auction yard in Los Angeles, where I hoped the salesman could identify the buyer of the armored truck.

It was four o'clock when I reached my office. I peeked in to say hi to Lucia, who was deluged with customers in a clothes-buying frenzy. I motioned to her I would be upstairs.

I typed up my notes, put them and the negatives into the wall safe, and stepped out the French doors onto the deck. The waves were crashing against the shoreline at unusual velocity, indicating a big storm on the way in. Suddenly, I got an idea.

I went back inside, rummaged through my purse for the business card Dr. Peterson had given me, and dialed his number.

"Sorry to trouble you, doctor, but this is Syracuse, up in Mendocino, and I need your help."

"Oh, yes, hello. I am so sorry to hear about Frank Spencer. I knew he was troubled, but I had no idea it was this serious," he said, concern in his voice. "But how can I be of help to you?"

"I need to find out who Billy's real father is. I know Frank Spencer wasn't, and I hoped you'd know who is. If I go through all the proper channels, it could take forever to get his name, and I don't exactly have a lot of time right now."

"I see. Well, Elizabeth told me his name, and I wrote it down in my notes. I'm not entirely sure it would be ethical, however, to give it to you."

"I could get a subpoena, but there's no time, doctor, and I'm afraid he might be involved in a lot of what's been going on up here."

"Yes, but wait, Anne knows his name; you could ask her."

"I can't," I lied. "I mean, I assumed she did, but I hate to bother her right now, you know?"

"Well, I'm coming up to Mendocino tomorrow night to see Anne and stay over for Frank's funeral. I have a room at the Mendocino Hotel. Why don't I bring the name with me and call you when I get there? Elizabeth's records are over at the hospital and I'm at my office now on the other side of town, so I won't be able to look it up until tomorrow. Can it wait that long?"

"Sure."

"O.K., talk to you then,' he said, and hung up.

Great. I could have sworn Anne said she didn't know the guy's name. Maybe Elizabeth told Peterson she's told Anne but hadn't. Shit! As Mark Twain once said, "Oh what a tangled web we weave, when first we practice to deceive." But who the hell was doing the deceiving here?

I walked back downstairs and stuck my head in Lucia's store. Several customers were lined up in front of the counter, charge cards in hand. I told Lucia I was feeling much better and would have dinner waiting for her when she got home. Her face brightened, as I knew it would, because she hated cooking.

After dinner, Harriet and Larry came over for a pinochle rematch. Out for revenge, they won the first two out of three games with a fast and furious attack.

CHAPTER 22

Early the next morning I called Ed to get the address of the place where Tony and Johnny had lived when they were arrested. It was several miles out Rolling Ridge Road, a notorious pot-growing region about forty-five miles northeast of Mendocino. Ed said the department had already been out there and hadn't found any heroin, if that was what I was looking for. I told him I wanted to snoop around anyway. He offered to go along, but I declined.

Economically, black tar heroin offered even higher profit margins than marijuana. I figured someone was picking up the heroin down at Noyo Harbor in Fort Bragg, or at an obscure landing site somewhere else along the coast, placing it in moneybags, and throwing it in the back of the armored truck. But then what? Even if the truck was a good cover-up for contraband, it seemed like gross overkill.

The boys' house was down a bumpy dirt road off an equally bumpy dirt road off the main ridge road. I meandered for miles through redwood forests recently clear-cut by logging companies. It was easy to see from the rapacious devastation why environmentalists were so alarmed by current logging practices. The latest political controversy was the lumber company's plan to ship un-milled lumber to Mexico and have it converted into redwood furniture by an inexpensive labor force, thus depriving local mill workers of their income, and then shipping the final product back to market in the United States. Political activists, a radical bunch on the coast, joined forces for once with the more conservative mill workers in this battle to stop the exportation of native raw lumber. A no-win situation, it was second only to the offshore oil drilling controversy, long a heated coastal issue.

My Volvo danced across the ruts and ridges in the road as I made the final descent to the boys' house. My sore rib felt like it had become disengaged from my ribcage, jiggled loose by the endless chuckholes. A red pickup was parked alongside the rustic cabin. There were no neighboring homes. I parked next to the truck, got out, and peered through the truck's dusty passenger window. The cab was empty except for several crumpled aluminum beer cans and a twisted pack of Camel cigarettes.

The front door of the cabin was ajar—no need for it to be secured, since it looked like Godzilla had picked it up, shaken it, and tossed it upside down to its final resting place. After picking through the debris for clues for half an hour and discovering nothing, I went back out to my car, flipped a U-turn, and headed back through the barren, clear-cut, former forest.

Depression crept into my psyche like fog overtaking the coast. Seeing the woeful remains of Tony and Johnny's cabin reminded me how senseless their deaths had been. They didn't even know what their botched up robbery was going to entail. Billy, another sad case of the apparently innocent victim getting caught in the crossfire, was also to be dutifully mourned. Maybe I was premenstrual, because at this moment, even though Spencer had always greeted me with the enthusiasm usually accorded insurance salesmen, a tear rolled down my cheek at the memory of his miserable demise.

At the same time, as if I didn't have enough to brood about, the ride out there re-ignited my passion to spend more time fighting for environmental causes. I was temporarily losing sight of my present focus in life, shifting my priorities from "my little investigation" to serious global concerns like saving the forests and oceans. Without them there would be no life, no detecting, no Grace Kelly beauties bursting through my door with intriguing stories.

When I got back to the office, my answering machine held a message from the salesman in Los Angeles, who said he thought he recognized one of the men in the photos I'd faxed him. He said he was faxing the picture back to me in care of the print shop I had used. I called the printer, but he said it hadn't arrived yet, in part because his machine was down for minor repairs, but he hoped to have it fixed late this afternoon or first thing in the morning.

Dr. Peterson had also called. Knowing I was anxious to learn Billy's father's name, he left it on the machine: it was Charles Walsh, a resident of Virginia. I remembered Anne saying she'd lived in Virginia, so it must have been during the family's stay there that her mother had had the costly affair.

I called information and learned there wasn't a phone listed for a Charles Walsh or a C. Walsh. My contact at the local DMV was next on my call list. He said he'd try to check with Virginia officials to see if the guy had a car registered in his name.

At five-thirty I went downstairs and stuck my head in Lucia's store to see if she wanted to go out for a bowl of soup, since neither of us cared to cook on too regular a basis. As we made our way over to the Mendocino Café, I told her about driving up Rolling Ridge Road.

"It's not enough you have a sniper after you, but then you waltz right into a notorious pot-growing region as if you're indestructible," she growled at me over the top of the menu.

"They've already harvested the pot for this season. No one would have been uptight at seeing me out there," I responded.

"You must be feeling better today—your arrogance is returning."

"I do. Your guest room had a great bed and I've been getting some deliciously sound sleep. Tank usually curls up on my head most of the night, so his absence makes me feel like I'm having regulation full nights of sleep, like regular people do who don't have irregular cats."

"Well, that doesn't mean you can remove that pretty vest yet; just because you're feeling perkier, don't get careless, which is a vague concept to you, I suppose," she said.

"Don't worry, I won't."

"Anything new with Anne's case?" she asked.

"Yeah. How'd you like to go to Virginia to visit your mother?"

"You *are* losing your mind," Lucia answered.

"Not entirely," I responded. "I think that's where Billy's father is and I'd like to have a talk with him. We could go together, and you could stay with your mom."

"I can't. It's almost Christmas, and I do run a retail business that's been crammed with crazed customers all week."

"I forgot."

"I thought you might have."

"Listen, don't wait up for me, I'm going to spend the night over at Ed's. I'll check in with you in the morning when I get to the office."

Lucia gave me a knowing grin. "That rib of yours must be feeling better," she said, raising her eyebrows slightly.

(HAPTER 23

Frank Spencer's funeral wasn't high on my list of social functions, but I felt it was my duty to Anne to show up, and also to check out the scene at the cemetery once again to see if anyone noteworthy crawled out of the woodwork to pay last respects to the pathetic, cantankerous banker.

Naturally, it poured for the duration of the service, which was attended by much of the same flock of black-umbrella-laden birds present just a short time ago at Billy's funeral. Noticeably absent was Elizabeth; I had to assume Dr. Peterson had made that choice, probably reasoning it would be the final upset that pushed her over the edge once and for all.

Ed and I had spent a very pleasant morning together, but he couldn't make it to the service due to a staff shortage at his office. I didn't notice any new faces besides Templeton the rat, whom I didn't remember seeing at Billy's funeral. He stood alone, left the cemetery unescorted by any of the other mourners, and walked down the hill to the same dark sedan I had noticed him in the night Sally Covington and I had been out on our fishing expedition.

Anne and Roger approached me afterward to see if I wanted to join them and Dr. Peterson for coffee at the Mendocino Hotel. We piled into separate cars and met in the hotel's sitting room in front of the warm, cozy fireplace.

Roger opened the conversation: "Where do you stand now with your investigation, Syracuse?"

"To tell you the truth, Roger, I'm not sure what direction to head in next. Frank's suicide certainly put a damper on things. I'm sure he knew something about this whole truck business, but of course he's taken his secrets to the grave."

Anne was next to Roger on one of the overstuffed couches, looking as if she'd taken an extra dose of the tranquilizers she'd acquired after Billy's death. Her face had a blank, static expression, like someone whose central nervous system was stuck in neutral. Her black wool dress only added to her emotionless affect.

I directed my attention to Dr. Peterson and asked, "Was Elizabeth too ill to attend the funeral?"

"I'm afraid so. She was in no shape to travel. I have her quite heavily sedated right now. You can imagine what the poor dear must be going through," he said.

Roger shifted in his seat and took a sip of his hot brandy. As if on cue, the rest of the entourage sipped from their glasses.

"So, what are you going to do, Syracuse?" Roger asked.

I looked over at Anne, who was as still as a hunted rabbit trying to fool its predator.

"Well, Roger, if Frank really was the mastermind behind this entire business, then he probably had a couple of thugs working for him, the guys dressed up in the fake guards' uniforms. My guess is, they're the ones who shot Tony and Johnny and then tried to kill me. Who they are is anybody's guess, and quite truthfully, I don't have any idea."

"Does the sheriff?" Dr. Peterson piped in.

"No. They do have some fingerprints though from when my office was broken into, and some from the armored truck, so if they belong to anyone who's been in trouble before, it might give us a lead."

"What about Billy's father?" Dr. Peterson asked.

Again I looked at Anne to check her reaction, but her face and eyes never changed expression.

"That's theory number two, the possibility that Frank was being blackmailed by someone from his past who planted the truck in his barn to incriminate him."

Roger looked at Anne and reached for her hand. He held it while he spoke. "I go along with that theory. I still can't believe Frank would be involved in anything the least bit illegal, and certainly not something as serious as murder."

"I must say I almost agree with you, Roger. Even though Frank and I didn't see eye to eye on most things, my gut feeling is he was a pretty decent guy and not the kind to get involved in criminal activities of this caliber. Cheat on his taxes, yes; kill people, no."

Even though Dr. Peterson knew I had Charles Walsh's name and hometown, I didn't want to tell the group I intended to go to Virginia and interrogate the guy. I needed to get back to the office, so I finished the last of my coffee and stood up.

"I really must be off." I looked over at Anne. She looked up at me and managed a small smile. "I'll be in touch," I added, heading for the door.

I walked the short distance to the office and climbed upstairs to my ocean-view perch. Settled at my desk, I called my Italian buddy, Joey Moretti, at the local travel agency a few doors down the street, booked a flight to Virginia, and reserved a rental car for tomorrow evening. I'd still have to drive my car as far as Ukiah to catch the airport shuttle bus to San Francisco. My DMV contact had one Charles Walsh in Virginia with a registered vehicle, so I now had a destination.

The print shop had left a message on my answering machine absolutely promising my fax from Los Angeles would be in sometime today.

Since it was late afternoon, but I still had at least two hours of daylight left, I decided to run out to my cabin, where I hadn't been to for days, and pack some clothes for my trip to Virginia. I reasoned that if the sniper was still lurking out there, he'd have as good a chance of firing at me wherever I was, so it shouldn't make any difference if I went to my own house, especially since it was still light.

Harriet was behind the counter when I walked down the steps past The Last Pimento. She was up to her elbows in curling ribbons and gift boxes, and had a long line of customers waiting to pay for their purchases. The Christmas rush was in full swing.

"Hi. I'm running out to my cabin for a few minutes to pick up some clothes. If anyone comes by, please tell then I'll be back in half an hour."

With a quick wave of her hand, she nodded her head and bestowed her classic, wide Harriet smile on me.

When I was halfway to my cabin the sun began to break through the clouds. Gentle waves lapped at the shoreline by Van Damme Beach, where several fishing boats had dropped anchor and sat swaying back and forth to the rhythm of the sea. From my vantage point, it still looked like the most romantic occupation one could have.

When I walked through the gate to my cabin, the late afternoon was still except for an occasional log truck passing on the road beyond, a recurrent rumble like an impending earthquake. It was steamy warm as the sun began to dry the bed of pine needles on the forest path, giving off a marvelously fresh, woodsy aroma. I felt at peace back in the sanctuary of my redwood cabin.

My mood was short-lived. Tank started reading me the kitty riot act outside the front door before I even had a chance to say hello. Even though he slept a good twenty-three hours each day, he expected to be doted on during his single hour of alertness, as if he were some religious icon to be endlessly adored. I could hardly blame him. I'd moved to Lucia's and he was alone—oh, so alone, by the sound of his pathetic meows.

Some eggs had been petrifying in the refrigerator, so I decided to make Tank a quick cheese omelet. I put on water for coffee, too, and went into the bedroom to pack a small suitcase.

CHAPTER 24

I hate flying.

I'd rather walk than face a trip confined in an aluminum can with wings. To be an airline passenger with an overactive, paranoid, and creative mind is among life's most difficult obstacles. It brings out every neurosis I have, and new ones emerge each time I make another pass at it.

Don't get me wrong: I'm fearless in other matters; I'm a private detective, for crying out loud, and live in greater danger than most people in most occupations, but flying is a whole different ballgame, you see, because I can't call any of the shots. I feel like a sitting duck in flight, strapped to a three-inch foam seat that's supposed to cushion the blow when we hit the ground from 50,000 feet straight up. I think it might help if I could sit in the cockpit.

Last time I flew, it was from San Francisco to Syracuse to attend my mother's funeral. There wasn't time to drive, much less walk there. On boarding the aircraft, I tried to remind myself I was a hotshot, semi-macho, private investigator who wasn't afraid of anything short of close-range machine gun fire, but as soon as the pilot revved the engines for takeoff at well over a hundred miles an hour, sweat gushed from every pore in my body in excess just short of a floodgate opening at the Hoover Dam.

This followed an earlier confrontation with the stewardess over the seating arrangements. I insisted on sitting in the back of the plane, next to the emergency door. She seemed to think that particular seat was reserved for her. Firmly, I said it was mine or else I wanted out. She gave in, but not before telling me the airline preferred to keep the back of the aircraft empty to help it balance better. The majority of the passengers were seated toward the middle of the plane, she said, and the flight attendants were seated in the back only during landings and takeoffs.

"Bullshit" was my assessment of her explanation, but once airborne and soaked in perspiration, I began contemplating her comment about balancing the plane by shifting the weight of the passengers uniformly. What about the baggage compartment? Did they also distribute *that* weight, so the silver bullet in the sky wouldn't suddenly flip over backwards in midair and send us somersaulting to our deaths?

Then I was sidetracked from my physics problem by a more imminent disaster, a flapping sound coming from one of the engines on my side of the plane. As the pilot increased speed, it got louder in range and pitch, resembling the sound effect I produced when I was a kid by using a clothespin to attach a baseball card to my bicycle fender; as the card made contact with the spokes, it sounded like an old muffler sputtering and coughing down the street.

Convinced something had broken off and fallen into the engine, I tapped the shoulder of the passenger in front of me, since there was no one beside me due to the weight problem we were experiencing, and asked him if he thought the noise was unusual. He said he couldn't hear it.

Flight attendants were busy passing out drinks, and many passengers were beginning to come to the rear of the plane to use the restrooms. A line started forming, a long line—some twenty people were now waiting to use the goddamn bathrooms, seriously upsetting the all-important weight distribution. What the hell did they know about aerodynamics? From my seat I searched the plane for the stewardess who had confided in me. She was nowhere in sight.

I thought maybe I should tell the passengers to remain in their seats until a bathroom became available, but I was afraid there would be mass hysteria if they knew our lives hung in such a delicate balance. Instead, I got up and took a leisurely stroll toward the front of the plane to counteract some of the weight differential until the line shortened.

When the coast was clear, I returned to my seat; just in time, too, because the pilot came on the sound system to tell us we were going to make an unscheduled landing to take on additional fuel.

This guy had to be kidding. Even a certified moron would know what he was saying: we'd run out of gas in mid-flight and were making an emergency landing, an emergency fucking landing. Cussing at myself for not having been more assertive with the ticket counter attendant about wearing a parachute, I clung to my seat cushion and wiped the sweat out of my eyes with my shirtsleeve. How fucking irresponsible to run out of gas in one of the nation's largest and, up until that moment, most prestigious airlines, in the middle of nowhere and some billion miles away from planet Earth. Christ, we were probably closer to Mars. Why the hell don't we land on fucking Mars? At least it might make the stop worth the inconvenience.

I knew we were in trouble when the stewardess began passing out free drinks during our "unscheduled landing," as if a drink would miraculously turn into a mini-parachute once the pilot pushed the ejection button, which I always felt should be required on commercial airlines, anyway. She gave me an ice-cream bar—big consolation for someone who's going to die in a fiery crash on the way to her own mother's funeral.

We landed safely, without a drop of fuel to spare, I'm sure. I tried to get off the plane and pick up a rental car, but we weren't allowed to disembark. I cursed the moron who'd forgotten to fill up our tank before we left San Francisco.

The engine continued to make the unnerving flapping sound, but at least we had fuel, so if we crashed we could have a nice big bonfire, maybe even roast marshmallows if anyone had thought to bring some along. Another hour passed and I held tightly to the idea that I had made a fatal error in having ever booked myself on this treacherous flight. I vowed that once off this flying coffin I would never fly again.

It was then that the first-rate pilot came back on the sound system to ask if there was a physician on board. Now I supposed the pilot was sick. Why not? What else could go wrong?

I wished there *were* a doctor on board; at this point I wasn't beyond asking him for a small dose of morphine to top off the ice-cream bar for the rest of the Godforsaken flight. The pilot came on a second time, asking for a doctor to assist a passenger who'd stopped breathing. *Stopped breathing! More air-line propaganda, for Christ's sake. This guy's in some kind of denial; everyone knows, when people stop breathing, they're dead, pal.*

Flight attendants circled around a passenger a few rows ahead of me, their faces white with fear. A gentleman in a dark suit seemed to be giving orders. I assumed he was a doctor. A few more moments passed and I saw one of the stewardesses cover the passenger's body and face—yes, face—with several skimpy airline blankets.

That was indeed the final straw for me, but what could I do, jump out the door to freedom? I rationalized my way into thinking nothing else could possibility go wrong now. We would make it to Syracuse; I could pay my last respects to my mother.

As we began our descent, the stewardess came over and sat next to me, strapping herself in securely. I made the mistake of asking her how things were going. She said fine, except the weather in Syracuse was lousy and would hinder her plans to go out that evening. Big deal, I thought, after what we'd just been through.

"Wind-chill factor of twenty below zero and white-out conditions," she added. I told her I wasn't really afraid to land in the snow because I knew the runways were heated to melt it away before we touched down. She gave me an incredulous look and said, "There's no such thing as a heated runway; they just throw a little sand on it for traction."

Oh, a little sand. How comforting.

We made it. Of course, we had to remain in our seats until the morgue attendants removed the body of the passenger who'd apparently had a fatal heart attack. "There for the grace of God go I" was about all I could say for the fiasco. After my mother's funeral, I rented a car and drove back to California.

Tank was rubbing against my leg, looking for some attention. I picked him up and put him under my arm while I walked across the room to the phone and called Joey at the travel agency. "Yes, you heard me right, I want to cancel my flight to Virginia. No, I don't care if my money won't be refunded."

I refused to share my neuroses with Joey, but I half suspected he knew why I was canceling, and didn't give a damn what he thought.

The coffee water was boiling, so I walked back into the kitchen to turn it off. Tank sauntered in, sensing I was once again within reach of the refrigerator. He wanted a little half-and-half to wash down his omelet.

I was grinding enough beans for two cups of strong java when my front door suddenly burst open and two figures lunged through the main room, heading for the kitchen. Fear shot through me like a jolt of electricity; my heart beat so fast it made my entire body jerk with its pounding. Instinctively, I crouched at the end of the U-shaped counter, but wasn't surprised when I saw their faces—and the drawn revolvers in their hands.

CHAPTER 25

"You don't look very surprised, my dear, just a bit startled by our unexpected visit, perhaps," Dr. Peterson said, some ten feet away, a menacing look on his face and a thirty-eight-caliber revolver pointed at mine.

"Yeah, I am a bit," I answered, in a cool, relaxed voice as if the situation I was presently in were commonplace.

"We didn't want to put you to the trouble of making that unnecessary trip to Virginia to see Mr. Walsh. He's not even real—just a name I threw out to buy a little time to plan my next move," Peterson continued. He kept his distance, remaining positioned just close enough to blow me away in a million pieces, standing flat-footed and alert to my every nuance. My bulletproof vest was no match for his gun.

"I picked up your fax for you on the way out here, Syracuse. You might say that was what prompted me to make this, uh, call," he said, handing me the fax.

With a thick marker, the guy at the auction yard had circled Peterson's face as the purchaser of the armored truck. I lowered my head and slowly shook it from side to side, trying to think of ways to buy time from this asshole.

"You really had me fooled, doc. I suspected Anne's husband more than anyone else in the case. I know this might seem a funny thing to ask you right now, considering the fact you're going to kill me, but I'm curious to hear just what the fuck this whole trip was about, y'know? I mean, I'd like to know before I, uh, die and all."

Peterson glanced over at his sidekick, Templeton the rat, as if to ask him if he minded if we talked for a few minutes. Templeton shrugged his shoulders in response, but kept his twenty-two aimed at me in case I was foolish enough to take the both of them on.

"You really didn't suspect me?" Peterson asked.

"No," I lied.

"Why did you ever think it was Roger?"

"Mostly because he's out of town a lot and travels to foreign countries where he could pick up heroin quite easily. I also bought the idea that Elizabeth's old lover might have been blackmailing Spencer," I answered.

I searched for signs of nervousness in Peterson, but he seemed calmly in control. He even looked dignified in his dark suit, tie, and overcoat. His eyes were steel blue, pupils dilated, his gaze cold as an Arctic wind. His hands looked like a doctor's: clean, hairless, and with long, delicate fingers like a piano player's, yet strong enough to brandish a large gun.

The rat, on the other hand, looked edgy, like he wanted to get on with the nasty task at hand, as impatient as Tank, drumming his fingers at his side with the hand that wasn't holding the twenty-two. Everything about him was mousy and ill kempt, from his face down to his feet, and his mannerisms were twitchy enough to make coffee nervous.

I looked around the kitchen, searching for a way out of my dilemma. Peterson stood at the end of the counter, blocking my escape route, and Templeton was just behind him and a little to the side. Tank was curled up on top of the refrigerator, eyes shut, asleep, I imagined, with not a cat care in the world—so much for his psychic abilities.

The phone rang, jarring both men and giving me hope that I could possibly be saved by the bell.

Peterson glared at me and said, "Don't answer it."

Four rings reverberated through the cabin before the answering machine kicked in and the voice on the other end said, "Hello, dear, this is Harriet. You said you were coming right back, so I just wondered where you were. I guess, uh, you've left, because you're not there, so I'll see you in a little bit. Ciao."

Christ, probably the last goodbye. I quickly tried to assess my situation, which looked pretty grim. My gun was in the bedroom next to my suitcase; I'd taken it off to try on a sweater to pack. That was dumb, in retrospect, if there's time for that in such a predicament, but it was also pretty stupid to leave the front door unlocked. The few extra seconds it would've taken then to break down the door might have been just enough for me to have gotten to my gun. The only weapon in reach was an eighteen-pound cat—about as lethal as the sponge on the sink.

"We don't have much time, Syracuse, your pals are starting to miss you already," Peterson said, an almost sadistic tone in his voice.

"So where do you fit into all of this?" I asked, wondering how many more precious seconds I could stall him.

"I'm a professional man, and I see that you too are a professional at what you do, so I will honor that and tell you the entire story before we must bid you farewell.'

"Oh, c'mon doc, let's get this over with and get outta here," Templeton piped in.

"Relax, Jonathan, we'll be out of here in a minute."

He turned to me and continued. "You see, Syracuse, I was Elizabeth's old flame, and Billy was my son," he said without emotion.

"I hardly know what to say," I answered, shocked at the thought of what was coming next.

Billy was a problem from day one. He never was a son to

me; I never felt any affection for him or any interest in his life. Spencer grew tired of his behavior, and poor Elizabeth was left to try to carry the burden herself. She never was very stable and Billy only added to her mental fragility."

Templeton was getting increasingly bored with our dialogue. He walked over to Tank's perch and started petting him. Good God. Worse yet, the damn cat purred—purred at the man who was going to kill the hand that fed him—and all the other body parts connected to it.

"When I discovered there was a lot, and I mean a tremendous amount, of money to be made in the heroin trade, I decided to enlist Frank's help. Naturally, he wasn't interested, because, you see, Frank was an honest man, a banker, a virtual pillar of the community, but once I explained I would spill the beans about Billy's conception, he began to soften, but not enough. Finally, I had to take Elizabeth away from him and hospitalize her in order to get some leverage."

"What do you mean?" I fired back.

"I mean that Elizabeth is being kept prisoner at the hospital. I have her medicated enough to keep her mouth shut, and she can't be released until I'm done with my trucking business, so to speak. Frank knew I would give her a convenient overdose if he squealed; Billy's fate was proof of that threat," he added.

Something dawned on me, something I'd suspected from the start and now proved true: one needle mark, perfectly placed, that was what the coroner said. Perfectly placed, as only a doctor could.

"You killed Billy."

"Now don't get me wrong, I never intended to kill Billy. It's just that he got in the way. In some ways he was too smart for his own good. He deduced that I was storing the heroin in the bank vault for safekeeping and that I brought it out to the barn until pickup could be arranged. I always removed it from the bank on Saturdays, when no one was around; that was the arrangement I had with Frank, but Billy went snooping around and discovered the entire operation. He began by just taking a little to sell on the side, but he got greedy. At the end he was going to start singing to you, so I had to get rid of him."

"So Frank wasn't really part of the operation?"

"No. That is, not a voluntary part. If he didn't go along with what I said, he knew I would kill Elizabeth."

"How did you get the heroin?" I asked, still hoping to string him out a few more minutes, until I could make a stab at an escape.

"It was brought in by boat to various secluded harbors along the coast. We'd pick it up in the armored truck. We used to take it directly to the barn before Billy started acting up, then we had to start stashing it in the vault."

"Did you do this in L.A. too?"

"No. It began when Frank moved up here to the boondocks where it was easy to bring the dope in."

I searched my mind for questions, anything to keep him talking until I was ready to make the only move I could. I was going to need a lot of luck and precise timing.

"What about Anne and Roger? Do they have any idea what's going on?"

"I don't believe so."

Suddenly the rat cut in: "C'mon, let's finish her off and get the hell outta here. Enough with the bullshit."

"Tie her up," the doctor ordered.

No way could I let that happen, no fucking way. I knew what he would do: inject me with one of his concoctions so it would look like I'd overdosed or died of natural causes. I couldn't let them restrain me.

"If I had my choice—" I blurted out.

"But you don't," Peterson responded.

"I don't have any rope, boss," the rat shot back. "I don't suppose we could borrow some, ma'am?"

That did it. In one swift movement I grabbed both the heavy iron skillet I had cooked Tank's omelet in and the pan of boiling water from the stove. I aimed one at each man, praying my left hand wouldn't let me down in time of need, and kicked the doctor in the groin as I ripped open his face—and probably broke his nose, by the sound of things—and covered the rat with the hot water. I had just enough time to jump over the far end of the counter and into my bedroom. I rolled across the bed, grabbed the gun, and slid to the floor on the far side of the bed. Both men burst through the door, guns firing.

Firmly gripping my pistol in both hands, I fired twice, hitting each of them neatly in the throat. They fell in a heap on the floor, much of the backs of their heads plastered against the white-enameled door, looking like spaghetti sauce and melted mozzarella as it dripped down the wood.

My heart was racing, and Tank was howling like I'd never heard him do before. Terror filled his eyes. He shot out the open front door and ran under the cabin just like he does during thunderstorms. I followed him out and fell to my knees in the front yard. Shaking and sobbing, I bent over and vomited several times.

Loud footsteps jerked me back to my senses. Ed was coming through the gate, his gun drawn.

"No need for that," I said.

(HAPTER 26

After spending more hours than I cared to at the sheriff's office being interrogated by Ed's boss, I was finally allowed to leave and drive out to Lucia's house. Ed sent a crew to my cabin to clean up what was left of the doctor and the rat, so I wouldn't have to face going home to a slaughterhouse.

Lucia had called Anne and Roger to meet us, and they were already there when I arrived. Ed was still with the sheriff.

Anne greeted me with a hug, full of celebration and thanks. Overjoyed at the outcome, she was eager to talk with me.

"As soon as I found out what Dr. Peterson was doing to mother, I stopped taking the medication he prescribed for me. He was overmedicating me, too," Anne said. "I'm still a little drowsy."

"I figured that," I said, pulling off my coat and walking toward one of the inviting couches. "How about some coffee, Lucia? That's what I was trying to make when those goons burst in."

"It'll be there in a sec, I'm just boiling some water," she answered from the kitchen.

"Syracuse," Roger piped in, "did you know it was Peterson all along?"

"Once I drove down to the hospital and saw the shape Elizabeth was in and the amount and kinds of drugs she was taking, he became suspect."

"I had no idea," Anne said, lowering her head.

"Why would you? We all grew up trusting doctors to some degree. This guy was a real smooth talker and a good con. The sheriff thinks he might have more than one woman like your mother, being held prisoner for his own gain through some scam or other. They're checking out that possibility right now."

I looked at Anne sitting in the oversized black chair across from me; radiant, elegant, relaxed, she was the essence of refinement.

"Peterson had a pretty good business going until Billy turned his friends on to the truck making its rounds every Saturday. It's ironic as hell that you just happened to be the one who spotted it, but on the other hand, it's not a well-traveled road, and you did live just a little way from the scene of the crime. Without your initial concern and bravery, Anne, this case might never have been investigated."

"And you believed me?"

"Yes, from the very start."

Lucia came into the living room bearing a tray with cups of coffee and cranberry scones from the Mendocino Bakery for all of us. I helped myself to two scones—I hadn't eaten all day.

"Why didn't you tell us your suspicions about the doctor sooner?" Roger asked.

"Didn't want to tip him off by thinking out loud. The less anyone knew, the safer they were. I needed more information, like the fax from L.A. I needed to build a solid case before blowing the whistle, and I thought I might also enjoy watching him hang himself. I bought his story about the Walsh guy in Virginia, though, but that was just a ruse."

"Mother's new doctor says it will be a few weeks before she can come home. He can't really evaluate her until all the medication has had a chance to wear off. Apparently, Dr. Peterson induced the majority of her problems by over-prescribing—she might be perfectly sane!" Anne said.

"He excelled at that," Roger added.

Lucia walked across the room to answer the ringing phone; it was Ed calling from the station. It seemed the sheriff was more interested in detaining him there than letting him drive out to be with us. Goddamn elected official! My hand clung to the receiver after I'd hung up, and an empty feeling gnawed at my stomach. Of all nights, this was one I wanted to spend with Ed, to revel in my victory together between soft flannel sheets.

I turned to Roger, who stood up and handed me a check; the amount was enough for me to live on comfortably for at least a year.

"What the hell's this for?" I asked.

"Anne and I talked it over. We can never repay you for all you've done for us. We can well afford this, so please accept it as your fee for the investigation. Take a vacation. You deserve it."

Visions of Sicilian beaches and stucco beachside homes with red-tiled roofs entered my mind. Palm trees swayed in the balmy breeze; no sound but the sea itself, aquamarine, like a large pool full of Grace Kelly's eyes.

"Syracuse?" Roger asked.

"Oh." I answered, coming to. "Thank you. Thank you so very much. I can assure you it will be put to very good use."

After discussing a few more details of the case, Anne and Roger left. Lucia came and sat next to me on the couch. We'd already talked at length at my cabin after the shootout, but I could sense she had more to add.

"When are you going to retire from this tedious detecting business of yours?"

"Are you serious?" I answered.

"Dead serious," she said, heavy emphasis on the first word.

"I like it."

"You're nuts."

"I'm alive, aren't I?"

"Barely."

A knock on the door put a sudden stop to her interrogation. In walked Harriet and Larry.

"Thanks for the call, H."

"You, my dear, had been gone way too long. I called Ed to go out there looking for you even before I called your cabin. I had a feeling something was up, because I saw the two thugs earlier. They were sitting in their car across the street from your office and pulled out to follow you when you left. What the hell happened to those eyes you're supposed to have in the back of your head?'

"You saved my life, Harriet."

"No, she didn't," Lucia screamed. "Your goddamn cat did."

"What the hell do you mean? Tank was asleep on the refrigerator the whole time. Let that jerk pet him. He's a two-timing traitor. He didn't do a goddamn thing to save me."

"If he wasn't so spoiled and hadn't insisted on having an omelet, you never would have had that frying pan on the stove. I know you; you hate to cook. It's probably the first time that pan's been out of the cupboard in years," Lucia announced.

"You've been talking to him, haven't you?" I whispered.

"I say this calls for a game of pinochle. What do you say?" Harriet chimed in.

The four of us looked at one another and nodded our heads in agreement.

"Why not? I'm on a roll. Deal 'em."